"Wishes Don't Come True If You Tell.

They're secrets of the heart."

"Do you have a lot of those? Secrets in your heart?" Steel asked.

"Do you?"

"Me? No." He smiled. "None."

"No hopes or dreams, Steel?"

"No, Megan," he said, his voice low, "I really don't. I just take life as it comes."

Steel's eyes swept over Megan's face. She stood perfectly still under his scrutiny, allowing it to warm her like brandy flowing through her veins.
Steel Danner was playing havoc with her mental equilibrium; he was dangerous to her well-ordered existence.

She wanted to scream at him to get out, but she dreaded the thought of his leaving. He filled the room with his vibrant masculinity, and she knew there would be a cloud of emptiness when he departed. Yes, he frightened her.

And he excited her.

Dear Reader,

Welcome to Silhouette! Our goal is to give you hours of unbeatable reading pleasure, and we hope you'll enjoy each month's six new Silhouette Desires. These sensual, provocative love stories are both believable and compelling—sometimes they're poignant, sometimes humorous, but always enjoyable.

Indulge yourself. Experience all the passion and excitement of falling in love along with our heroine as she meets the irresistible man of her dreams and together they overcome all obstacles in the path to a happy ending.

If this is your first Desire, I hope it'll be the first of many. If you're already a Silhouette Desire reader, thanks for your support! Look for some of your favorite authors in the coming months: Stephanie James, Diana Palmer, Dixie Browning, Ann Major and Doreen Owens Malek, to name just a few.

Happy reading!

Isabel Swift
Senior Editor

SDRL-7/85

ROBIN ELLIOTT
Pennies in the Fountain

Silhouette Desire

Published by Silhouette Books New York

America's Publisher of Contemporary Romance

SILHOUETTE BOOKS
300 East 42nd St., New York, N.Y. 10017

ISBN: 0-373-05275-8

First Silhouette Books printing April 1986

America's Publisher of Contemporary Romance

Printed in the U.S.A.

ROBIN ELLIOTT

lives in Arizona with her husband and three daughters.
Formerly employed in a high-school library, she is now
devoting her time to writing romance novels. She also
writes under her own name, Joan Elliott Pickart.

For Kit Kolb Dee,
who listens, and listens, and . . .

One

Steel Danner accepted the embossed menu from the waitress and glanced at it quickly, placing an order for coffee, apple pie and a glass of milk—his standard fare for all occasions. His ebony eyes flickered over the plush interior of the restaurant, scanning the faces for the one he sought.

Nothing. Just a bunch of idle rich people whiling away the afternoon before wandering off to expensive homes, country clubs or wherever the mood and their wallets took them. What Steel Danner wanted to do was loosen the necktie that was strangling him. He hated ties. He'd decided long ago that they'd been invented by a woman who was seeking revenge on the male population. But to get into this snobby place one had to wear a tie; so he would have to suffer.

Steel's order was placed in front of him, and he mumbled his thanks, looking up at the waitress when she asked if there was anything else.

"No, this is fine," he said, flashing her a dazzling smile that revealed white teeth against his bronzed skin.

"Your check," she said, then turned and walked away.

Steel shrugged and took a bite of his pie. Definitely not a friendly waitress, he thought. They probably had rules in this place about flirting with the customers. Oh, well, he didn't have time for that stuff today anyway.

Steel slowly consumed his pie, which, he decided, had a soggy crust and wasn't worth the outrageous price the restaurant was charging. He gave the impression of being relaxed, at ease, as if he didn't have a worry in the world. In actuality, he was coiled, tense. His dark eyes swept the room, and a muscle twitched in his jaw. With large hands that had long, tapering fingers, he lifted the coffee cup to his lips and peered over the rim at the people moving in and out of the restaurant. Nothing. The person he was searching for wasn't there.

Steel shifted in his chair, wide shoulders bunching under the sport jacket he wore over a pale-blue dress shirt. Dark slacks pulled against muscled thighs, and he swore silently at the latticework on the back of the chair that dug into his spine. Wonderful. Not only was he being strangled by his necktie, he was getting puncture wounds in his back!

Steel returned his cup to the saucer and reached for his glass of milk, but his hand stopped in midair, then came to rest flat on the table. A woman was walking toward him, following the maître d', who was showing her to a table about ten feet away from Steel. She nodded her approval and sat down, crossing her legs and smoothing the skirt of her silky yellow dress.

Now *those* were legs, Steel thought. Long, shapely legs, trim at the ankles and accentuated by high heels. His eyes traveled upward past the gentle curve of the woman's hips and small waist to linger on full breasts pushing against the lush material of her dress. Strawberry-blond hair fell to her shoulders in loose waves. Nice chin, kissable lips, pert nose and large eyes, though their color was indiscernible from his vantage point.

Classy. Every inch of her said money, breeding and class. And she was waiting for someone. She glanced continually at the entrance and shook her head when the waitress approached to take her order.

Steel redirected his attention to his milk and downed the cool liquid in two swallows. Now what? he wondered. He'd run out of stuff to eat. Stall. Signal the waitress for more coffee and ignore the pain in his back and the stranglehold on his neck. His gaze traveled again to the entrance and then over to the strawberry blonde, whose eyes had taken the same journey in his direction.

As their eyes met, Steel felt as though he had been punched in the stomach. There was no readable expression on her face; she was simply looking directly at him. He registered a sense of expectancy, an anticipation of what would come. A coy lowering of her lashes? He waited, his gaze meeting hers steadily, unwavering, and an aeon seemed to pass. And still she did nothing but look at him.

Steel swore silently as he felt the heat shoot through him. What was it with her? She wasn't even moving and she was getting to him. Hell, he'd had enough of this! He was there for a purpose, and it didn't include games with some rich society woman. Damn, she was pretty. What color were those magic eyes of hers?

Steel tore his gaze away and concentrated on the door. A trickle of sweat ran down his back and he felt an uncomfortable pressure against his zipper. The woman was a witch! Steel Danner didn't get turned on by looking at a female across a room! It was the necktie. It was cutting off the oxygen to his brain.

"More coffee?" the waitress asked.

"Yeah, thanks, honey," Steel said, and was rewarded by a giggle, which made him feel halfway normal again.

Megan James watched the waitress pour more coffee for the man across the room and only then realized that her hands were trembling. She quickly placed them on her lap and studied the carnations in the vase in the center of the table.

Something had happened to her when her eyes had met those of the man. She'd been mesmerized, held immobile, hardly able to breathe. Her own heartbeat had echoed in her ears. His eyes were black velvet as was the thick hair combed heavily over his ears and falling to the collar of his jacket. He was big, tall, appeared strong and exuded a blatant sexuality that had reached out to her despite the distance between them. Skin bronzed by the sun, and perhaps by heritage, covered his high cheekbones, square chin and straight nose. His lips knew kissing, she guessed, knew...

What was she doing? she wondered. This was crazy! What expression had crossed her face as they had stared at each other? Oh, dear heaven, she hadn't sent some sordid signal had she? No, apparently not, as he'd made no move toward her. But those eyes! From where she was seated, his eyes seemed like fathomless pools of darkness that had swallowed her senses as she drowned in their depths. And there she'd sat, gawking at him like an adolescent. Incredible. She'd never done anything so ridiculous before. Oh, damn the man and his nonstop body. And damn his raven eyes!

Steel sipped his coffee and frowned, causing his dark eyebrows to draw together. He was running out of time. He couldn't nurse the coffee much longer without becoming conspicuous. Ten more minutes and he'd have to leave.

With as much pull as a magnet on metal shavings, Steel's eyes were drawn once more to the woman. She was studying the flowers in the milk-glass vase in the center of the table as if they were the most fascinating things she had ever seen. What color were her eyes? With that hair, maybe blue? Green? Milk-chocolate brown?

"Ah, hell," he muttered under his breath as he stared into his cup again. Five more minutes and then he was getting out of there.

Suddenly Steel stiffened, his body taut, coiled like a panther ready to spring. There was no change in the slightly bored expression on his face, no noticeable difference in the way he sat in the uncomfortable chair, but every muscle in his body was tensed, ready.

He had just come in the door.

Frankie Bodeen.

The man was fifty, balding and wearing a five hundred dollar white suit. It was definitely Frankie Bodeen. A pulse beat in the thick column of Steel's neck, and he clenched his jaw until it ached as the maître d' led Bodeen to the table where the strawberry blonde was seated.

Damn, Steel thought, snatching his check off the table and pushing himself to his feet. And he'd thought she had class. There was nothing classy about a woman who hung out with Frankie Bodeen!

Steel left the restaurant and immediately tugged off his tie, stuffing it in his pocket. While undoing the top button of his shirt, he glanced around for a secluded spot where he could watch the door. Weaving his way through the traffic, he crossed the street and positioned himself in the shadows cast by a canopy overhanging a boutique. Folding his arms loosely over his broad chest, he leaned against the building...and waited.

Steel Danner knew how to wait. He had the skill of separating his mind into sections; one part intent on the mission at hand, the other on any mental ramblings he chose to pursue. It was an old Indian trick, a product of the teachings of his grandfather, and it had held him in good stead.

But today the fanciful part of his consciousness saw only long satiny legs, full breasts, reddish-blond hair and eyes of a mysterious color. He saw a steady gaze that had held him pinned in place and caused the blood to run hot in his veins. He saw lips as soft as rose petals that would move seductively against his own. She was fairly tall, maybe five-six without her fancy shoes, and looked about twenty-six or -seven. Damn, what color were her eyes? And what was she doing with a creep like Bodeen?

Steel muttered an expletive and shifted his weight restlessly before settling back against the wall. The Los Angeles atmosphere was heavy with yellowish smog that hung low over the city. The April weather was nondescript; not hot, not cold, just there.

A girl walked by, giving Steel a wide smile, and he winked at her for the lack of something to do. Women liked Steel Danner, always had, and he liked women. He never phonied up, never made promises he didn't intend to keep, never lied to them. He admired and respected women, but he sure as hell wouldn't want to be married to one.

Steel's thoughts skittered again to the woman in the restaurant, and he scowled, his dark eyes cold. He'd paid twenty bucks to an informant who'd sworn Bodeen would surface today to make an important contact at the swanky establishment. For eight months Steel and his partner, Casey, had been after Bodeen. They'd hauled in more drug users and two-bit pushers than they could count, but could never get anything solid to pin on Bodeen. That lowlife ran more drugs through L.A. than all the small dealers put together, and they couldn't nail him. Bodeen was smart. He covered his tracks and strutted his stuff, and Steel hated his guts. Today, the informant had said, Frankie was setting up a big one and was meeting his man at the restaurant.

Man? Hell, Steel thought with a snort of disgust, that long-legged beauty was no man. The strawberry blonde was a drug dealer? All of his instincts screamed no, but anything was possible. Miss Witch Eyes could be in on it up to her cute little nose. Either that, or his contact had ripped him off and the woman was Bodeen's afternoon entertainment. Damn, the thought of Bodeen's fat hands on her infuriated him.

The expletive Steel ground out caused an elderly woman to frown and click her tongue.

"Excuse me, ma'am," Steel said, smiling at her engagingly. "My old war wound is acting up. Terrible pain. Terrible."

"Oh, you poor dear," she said. "I do hope you'll feel better."

"Thank you, ma'am. You're most kind. I'm very sorry I said that nasty word. Believe me, my mother wouldn't approve. Have a nice day."

"You, too, dear," she said, walking away.

Steel chuckled softly, leaned back against the wall . . . and waited.

An hour later, Steel stiffened and moved completely out of view along the edge of the building. Bodeen emerged from the restaurant with his hand resting on the woman's elbow, and they walked to the edge of the curb. Bodeen raised his hand, and a limousine came from around the corner and stopped in front of them.

She was Bodeen's afternoon delight, Steel thought, narrowing his eyes. Fancy lunch and now off they went for a romp in the hay. How could a woman like that allow herself to be touched by the likes of Frankie? Well, well, well, look at that.

Bodeen got into the back seat of the car, and it sped away as the woman turned and walked down the sidewalk, her long legs carrying her in a fluid, graceful motion. A small smile tugged at the corner of Steel's mouth as he moved out of the shadows and started across the street. But the smile slid off his chin and was replaced by a twitch in his jaw.

So, okay, she wasn't a high-priced call girl, he thought, which put him back to square one. She could be Bodeen's new contact for whatever was going down and into drugs all the way up to her voluptuous bazooms. He'd better take a closer look at Miss Witch Eyes with the strawberry-blond hair.

Steel followed the woman for six blocks as she strolled leisurely along the sidewalk, stopping to gaze into store windows before moving on again. She had a habit of fluffing her hair with her hand when she leaned closer to inspect an item on sale, and a breeze blew her dress tightly against the sloping curve of her body. Steel saw it all, every detail, and again wondered absently what color her eyes were.

At last the woman cut across a small park, and Steel hung back, not wanting to be caught in the open. He moved behind a row of large trees and saw the woman stop in front of a fountain, withdraw a coin from her purse and drop it into the water.

What had she wished for? he thought. A nice fat cut of the pie from Bodeen? A smooth-running drug transaction that would blow the cops' minds because they couldn't catch anyone red-handed? Hell, it was a desecration of a wishing fountain. Those were for whimsical dreams of true love and happiness. Was anything sacred these days?

Steel felt his sharp intake of breath as the woman ran her fingertips under the spraying water. She cocked her head to one side like a little girl, then placed one finger in her mouth to taste the cool liquid. It was a seemingly innocent gesture on her part, but it was erotic, totally feminine, and a knot tightened in Steel's stomach.

The woman continued her journey through the park, crossed a narrow cobblestone street and entered a shop on the other side. Steel's eyes flickered over the sign done in old English script: Memory Lane.

"Hello, Clara," Megan said as she entered the store, "Everything all right here?"

"Just fine. Mrs. Wilson called and said she wants the brass candlesticks after all. I wrapped them and put them on the shelf in your office with her name on them."

"Excellent. Off you go to lunch."

"Okay, see you later."

In the now quiet store, Megan allowed the tranquility to wash over her as she strolled among the attractively arranged antiques. Everything was perfect, and it was hers. All hers. The hard work and long grueling hours had paid off, and Memory Lane was showing a bigger profit every month. She had gained a reputation for having fine quality at reasonable prices, and she had done it all herself. She'd fought tooth and nail for the bank loan five years ago to get started and had repaid every cent. The first cramped quarters had been replaced by better, then a year ago she had moved here to an affluent neighborhood and established herself among the wealthy.

And they came. In their Rolls-Royces and Mercedes they came to *her* store, to buy *her* beautiful antiques, and boasting to their friends about the marvelous items they had found at the exclusive Memory Lane. She had arrived. And, by God, she was staying! She had even been sent to Paris by one of her clients to purchase a special piece, and other patrons were hinting at European trips in the future. The world was hers!

Megan moved behind the counter and wiped the fingerprints off the top with a soft rag. When the old-fashioned bell above the door tinkled, she looked up with a smile and then gasped. It was him! she thought wildly. The man from the restaurant, whom she had stared at like some kind of hussy. Oh, dear heaven, she *had* sent him some kind of message with her long steady gaze, and whatever he thought she was offering he was there to collect! She had to stay calm, cool, and send him on his way!

"Hello," she said, a stiff tilt to her chin. "May I help you?"

Green, Steel thought, walking slowly toward her. Her eyes were the most remarkable shade of clear, sparkling green he'd ever seen. Emeralds. Yeah, that's what they reminded him of. Did they turn smoky like jade when she was filled with desire? "Hello," he said, clearing his throat roughly. "Nice place. Yours?"

"Yes."

"Catchy name, Memory Lane."

"I like it," she said. He was beautiful, she thought. He was the most ruggedly handsome man she'd ever seen. Those eyes! They were so black she could hardly distinguish the pupils. He was tall, over six feet, and moved with an easy rolling gait, but there was strength in his body that was being held tightly in check. He radiated power, both physically and with a sense of authority. This man was dangerous.

"So," Steel said, leaning against the counter, "how would you like to play this?"

"I beg your pardon?"

"I can pretend I just happened to walk in here, or we can admit we saw each other in the restaurant. What suits your fancy?"

"Why did you follow me?"

"Because I had to know what color your eyes were."

"You waited outside all that time and trailed after me to see my eyes?"

"Yep."

"That's ridiculous."

"No, it's not. You have very lovely eyes. Green."

"I know they're green," Megan said sharply. "Look, I'm afraid I gave you the wrong impression in the restaurant. I realized I was staring at you but I—"

"Danner. Steel Danner. Who are you?"

"Megan James. Mr. Danner, I—"

"Steel. You have a pretty name. It suits you, Megan James."

"Mr. Danner—"

"Steel."

"I don't wish to be rude, but I've already explained that I meant nothing by the fact that I looked at you the way I did. I think it would be best if you left my store."

"Why? Is your boyfriend due?"

"Boyfriend?"

"The hot dog you had lunch with."

"He's not my boyfriend," she said, bursting into laughter. "Oh, ugh, give me a break."

A startled expression flitted across Steel's face and then a smile. Megan's laughter lilted through the air and danced up his spine. She was without a doubt the loveliest woman he'd ever seen. "Yeah, well," he said, "so the money man isn't your boyfriend."

"No, he isn't," she said. His whole face had changed when he'd smiled, she thought. His features had softened and his eyes had been warm, sooty black instead of dark pools like the devil's own. Who was this man, this Steel Danner? Steel. It was the perfect name for him. Sharp, cold steel, but steel would warm when held in a hand, when gently held so one wasn't hurt by cutting edges. What fanciful thoughts. She didn't even know him!

"I'm glad to hear that," Steel said, nodding. "He wasn't your type. So why were you with him?" Easy, Danner, he thought. Don't push it.

"Business."

"Whatever," he shrugged, then pushed himself off the counter to wander slowly around the store. Business? Yeah, right. Drugs were very big business. Damn, she didn't fit the image of a dealer, and it wasn't just her looks. It was something else; an underlying vulnerability, a gentleness. If she was mixed up with Bodeen, she was way out of her league. Bodeen would manipulate her, use her and then throw her away. "What's this?" Steel asked, picking up a spoon.

"A spoon."

"I can see that," he said, smiling at her over his shoulder. "What's the big deal?"

"It belonged to Martha Washington."

"I'll be damned," he said, placing it carefully back in the blue velvet-lined case. "Ol' George slurped his soup with that very spoon, huh?"

"Somehow, Mr. Danner," Megan said, laughing, "I get the feeling you don't appreciate antiques."

"It's Steel, Megan," he said, walking back to the counter. "Steel."

"Steel," she said softly.

Neither of them moved, nor hardly seemed to breathe as their eyes met and held. Steel felt the sweat trickle down his back again, the gun in his shoulder holster suddenly heavy as a shaft of heat shot across him.

The air seemed to swoosh from Megan's lungs as a roaring started in her ears. Her heart raced, and she was drowning; drowning in the fathomless depths of Steel Danner's eyes. She should move, but couldn't. Wanted to, but didn't. A honeyed warmth began to spread throughout her, causing a flush on her cheeks. She felt feminine and alive and, under Steel's mesmerizing gaze, even beautiful. She was a woman. And, oh, dear heaven, never before had she met such a man.

"Are you a witch, Megan James?" Steel said, tracing his thumb lightly over her lips. "What is this spell you're casting over me?'' Lord, her lips were soft, but he'd known they would be. Damn, he wanted to kiss this woman!

Megan blinked once slowly as Steel's work-roughened thumb grazed her lips. And *his* lips? she thought. What would they feel like on hers?

"Steel," she said, taking a step backward and shaking her head slightly, "don't. Just don't."

"Do I frighten you, Megan?" he asked, shoving his hands into his pockets. "Because I'll tell you something. You scare the hell out of me, lady. Are you sure you're not a witch?"

"Positive," she said as she laughed, finally breaking the crackling tension between them.

"Well, thank God for that much," he said, smiling at her warmly. Damn! Why had she been with Bodeen?

"It happened again," Megan said. "Your smile leaves your eyes and they become so cold, like...steel. Is that where you got your name? Because of your eyes?"

"No," he said chuckling, the sound rich and throaty. "It's short for something else."

"Oh?"

"Blade of Steel," he said, looking directly into her green eyes.

"I beg your pardon?"

"I'm half Hopi Indian. My name is Blade of Steel Danner. *Now* do I frighten you?"

"Because you're an Indian? No. Because you're a very intimidating man? Yes."

"Intimidating? Me?" he said, covering his heart with his hand. "Really, Miss James, you're hurting my feelings. I'm a laid-back, easygoin' guy."

"No, Mr. Blade of Steel Danner," she said laughing, "you are not."

"Ah, man, I like it when you laugh. It's like wind chimes. What did you wish for when you threw the coin in the fountain?"

"You saw me do that?"

"Yeah, you looked like a little girl," Steel said. "What did you wish for?" Something about Bodeen? No, damn it!

"Wishes don't come true if you tell. They're secrets of the heart."

"Do you have a lot of those? Secrets in your heart?"

"Do you?"

"Me? No," he said smiling. "None."

"No hopes or dreams, Steel?"

"No, Megan," he said, his voice low, "I really don't. I just take life as it comes."

Steel's eyes swept over Megan's face. She stood perfectly still under his scrutiny, allowing it to warm her like brandy flowing through her veins. Steel Danner was playing havoc with her mental equilibrium; he was dangerous to her well-ordered existence. She wanted to scream at him to get out, but dreaded the thought of his leaving. He filled the store with his vibrant masculinity, and she knew there would be a cloud of emptiness when he departed. Yes, he frightened her. And he excited her. He was heaven and hell in a six-foot-plus package, and she had to break free of the sensual web he was weaving around her. She had to!

"Steel, I really must get to work," she said, picking up the dust rag and wiping the counter. "It was nice meeting you."

"That counter is not the only thing getting dusted off here," he said, frowning. "I take it I'm being dismissed?"

"I have a business to run," she said, not looking at him.

"Right," he said tightly. And the business with Bodeen? When did she plan to get started on that? "I'll see you around."

"Goodbye," she said, slowly lifting her eyes to look at him.

Steel stared at her for a long moment, then turned and strode out the door without a further word, his jaw set in a tight, hard line.

Megan drew a shuddering breath and on trembling legs walked into her office and sank into the chair behind her desk. Steel. Blade of Steel, she thought. He had consumed her senses, and his image danced before her eyes as she closed them, her fingertips pressed to aching temples. Well, now he was gone and she'd dismiss him from her mind. One foolish act in a crowded restaurant had turned her world upside down, but now he was gone. He'd been angered by her sudden coolness and he wouldn't be back.

Fine. Men like Steel Danner were used to getting whatever they wanted. Steel was a user, a taker, with no hopes or dreams. He lived for today and took what he wanted from it. He would not have Megan James!

Steel stalked across the street and through the park, stopping suddenly in front of the fountain and raking his hand through his thick hair. Megan, he thought. Which of those coins had she thrown in there and what had she wished for? Who was Megan James and what was her connection with Frankie Bodeen? And why in the hell was Steel rendered off balance each time he looked into those incredible green eyes?

"You're losing it, Danner," he muttered, starting back in the direction of the restaurant to retrieve his car. "She wasn't *that* terrific."

On impulse Steel spun around and went back to the fountain, pulling a coin from his pocket and flipping it into the water. For the life of him, he couldn't think of one thing to wish for and, for some unknown reason, that fact covered him in a cloak of depression.

Megan pushed herself to her feet and walked through the quiet store to stare out the window at the fountain across the street in the park. It was a daily ritual, her penny in the fountain. A silent plea from the recesses of her soul that her world would not crumble around her and be blown away like dust from the palm of a hand. She'd worked her way out of a lonely life with few opportunities, nothing, *nothing*, would take from her what she now had. The sorrow was years ago and yesterday in one jumbled mass in her mind.

When Steel had looked at her so intently, what had he seen? she wondered. A woman of breeding, of class, elegance? Or had those ebony eyes swept beyond the facade? Never had a man studied her so thoroughly as if stripping her bare, not only of clothing, but of her protective walls as well. No, her imagination was running away with her. She'd acted foolishly in the restaurant and issued an invitation to a rich playboy on the make. Well, Steel was gone now and wouldn't return.

But it was just as she'd expected.

The store seemed very, very empty.

Two

Steel drove the three-year-old dark sedan out of the restaurant parking lot and down Wilshire Boulevard. He was hungry, he thought. Starved. Soggy pie was not exactly a thrilling lunch, and he definitely needed some food.

After several miles, Steel turned and drove slowly through a residential area consisting of upper-middle-class homes. The driveway he pulled into was next to a large two-story house, and his gaze swept over the perfectly manicured lawn as he approached the front door and rang the bell. A few moments later the door was flung open and a woman smiled up at him.

"Steel!" she said. "What a nice surprise. Come in."

"Hello, pregnant person," he said, kissing her on the cheek as he entered the living room. "How are you?"

"Fat!"

"True. I swear, Roddy, I'm going to have to haul you in for smuggling bowling balls. Hi, *Tiposi*," he said, patting the woman's protruding stomach. *"Um wayn-uma?"*

"He's *very much* in there," Roddy said, laughing.

Steel leaned over and leveled his nose with Roddy's stomach. *"Nú as uukwatsini.* Okay, kid?"

"Come on, you crazy Indian," Roddy said, smiling. "Quit speaking Hopi to my unborn child and tell me what I've done to deserve the honor of your company in the middle of the day."

"I'm trying to improve my nephew's vocabulary," Steel said. "And I'm hungry."

"Should have known. Food. Let's go in the kitchen."

Steel circled the pretty woman's shoulders with his arm as they walked to the rear of the house and entered the kitchen. Roddy came up to his shoulder and had two long, dark braids streaming down her back. Her skin was bronzed like Steel's and her eyes were large and dark and danced with merriment when a smile lit up her lovely face.

"You don't look so hot, Waving Goldenrod," Steel said.

"You're so good for my morale. Sit."

"Hey, I can fix my own if you're tired or something, sister mine."

"No way. I'd be another hour cleaning up after you. Sit!"

"Whew!" Steel said, sitting on a chair. "Pregnant women are grouchy."

"Why the sport coat? You look so cute."

"Cute? Wonderful. Every thirty-six-year-old man wants to be known as cute. I was rubbing elbows with the filthy rich, for your information. Crooks come in all tax brackets. How's Brian?"

"Fine. He can hardly wait to be a father," Roddy said, placing a plate with two large sandwiches in front of Steel. "I'll get your milk."

"Pick names yet?" Steel asked, then took a big bite of his sandwich.

"No! Brian wants to use Indian names and I refuse. No child of mine is getting stuck going through life as Waving Goldenrod or Blade of Steel. Honestly, Brian is so silly."

"Blade of Steel," Steel said thoughtfully. "Roddy, do you think I have cold eyes?"

"What?" she asked, sitting opposite him.

"My eyes, are they cold? Someone asked me if I was called Steel because of my eyes."

"Well, it's hard to explain. When you smile and really mean it, your eyes are warm, kind of soft. But you've seen so much pain in your life that you have a way of looking right through a person like you can see their soul. And when you're angry? Yes, your eyes are as cold as steel. You probably don't need to carry that gun. You could stare at a criminal and scare him to death. Grandfather says you have eyes of many faces."

"Eyes of many faces?"

"That's what he told me once. He said you mirror your feelings in your eyes. Who was this person who remarked about your name? A woman?"

"Yeah," he said, draining his glass and refilling it.

"She's very perceptive. Someone special?"

"No."

"They never are. You love 'em and leave 'em," Roddy sighed. "That's partially my fault. Think of the years you spent watching over me. You were more like a father than a brother. I still feel so badly about the way I conducted myself when I first came to L.A. I was so caught up in my fancy new modeling career and was running with that wild party crowd, and—"

"That's all behind you, Roddy. Forget about it."

"Steel, you know everything changed when I met Brian. I got back in touch with myself, knew I wanted the world Brian was offering me. We're so in love, we're about to have a baby and I'm so happy. But don't you see? I robbed you of the chance to lead your own life. Your time was spent hovering around, pulling me out of situations I didn't belong in, literally protecting me from myself. What about your need for love, for a commitment to a woman who can make you happy?"

"You haven't deprived me of anything, Roddy," he said, shaking his head. "I have no desire to get married or settle down. I'm going to spoil your kid rotten. That's good enough for me."

"One of these days you're going to fall in love, Blade of Steel."

"Not me. I'm immune to the disease. I've got to go. Thanks for the lunch, Roddy."

"Bye, Steel. I love you."

"*Tsangawpi'i. Adiós.*"

"*Adiós?* That's Spanish."

"I'm a well-rounded guy. Talk to you later."

"Bye," Roddy said as Steel left the room. "I wonder who the woman is that understood his eyes of many faces?"

Megan finished packing a vase for shipping and then poured herself a cup of coffee before sinking wearily into her chair behind her desk.

Steel Danner. Every effort to push him from her thoughts had failed. His image was there with her: tall, strong, golden like a statue. She had never been so rattled, both physically and emotionally by a man. He had swept across her senses, and she felt shaken, threatened. She knew she was acting foolishly. Steel was merely a man who had time to waste and had decided to follow up on what he had thought had been an invitation issued by an available woman. When she hadn't proven to be an easy pickup, he'd moved on to greener pastures. She would never see him again and that was fine with her.

Those eyes, she thought. Those ebony eyes had been her undoing. So warm and in the next instant so chilling, Steel's eyes had touched her in a place deep within herself. Fingers of desire had danced across her body under his scrutiny, and she had felt alive as if awakening from a lifelong slumber. The soft brush of his thumb across her lips had kindled a flame within her, and his eyes had been warm, soft, promising. And then cold. Cold as steel.

It was fitting that Steel Danner was an Indian. Blade of Steel. Yes. He moved with the gracefulness, the tight control of his ancestors. He was like the mountain lions his forefathers had stalked: strong, smart, his power held in check until the exact moment he chose to spring forth and unleash it. He could not be tamed, not Steel; he would have to be free, left alone to live his life under his direction, his control.

"Go away, Steel Danner," Megan said, pressing her fingertips to her temples. "Get out of my head and leave me alone!"

As Steel pulled into the parking lot at the police station, he concentrated on Frankie Bodeen. Bodeen. Megan. Lovely, green-eyed, long-legged Megan James, who was playing with fire in Bodeen's cruddy world, and who was going to get burned.

Inside the building, Steel walked down a narrow corridor and opened a door to an office housing several computers and a double row of filing cabinets.

"Howdy, Cochise," a uniformed officer said. "I presume you want something for free?"

"Yep, Paleface," Steel said. "Run a check on Megan James for me, will ya?"

"When do you need it?"

"Yesterday."

"Always. You Indians are not patient people. I'll bring it over to your office."

"You're ever so kind."

"Why the fancy jacket? Getting married?"

"Fat chance. See ya."

Steel made his way back down the hall and entered a large room jammed with desks and milling with people, some in civilian clothes, others in uniforms. Wolf whistles, catcalls, hoots and hollers greeted his arrival.

"Hey, Steel, who died? Been to a funeral?"

"Trade your bow and arrow for that jacket, Steel?"

"What's up, Geronimo? Posing for a centerfold?"

"Okay," Steel said, grinning, "knock it off. General Custer was a smart mouth, too, you hot dogs, and look what happened to him. Casey around?"

"In that pigsty you two call an office," a man said. "Yes, your partner Julian is in attendance."

"Julian?" Steel said quizzically. "You *are* living dangerously today."

"You will notice I didn't say it where he could hear it. He'd mess up my beautiful face."

"'Tis true," Steel said, nodding as he headed down the hall.

He stopped off in a small kitchen, retrieved a quart of milk from the refrigerator, then entered the office he shared with his partner, Casey Jones.

"Lieutenant Danner," Casey said, "nice of you to drop by. I take it the boys out front fully appreciated your fine attire?"

"Ate it up," Steel said, shrugging out of his jacket and placing his gun on his desk.

Steel and Casey had been partners for five years and had saved each other's life on more than one occasion. They worked well together, thought alike and respected each other as men as well as police officers. Casey was five-foot-ten with sandy-colored hair and a tightly muscled physique. Married, he was the father of four-year-old twin boys. He wanted to nail Frankie Bodeen as badly as Steel Danner did.

"Bodeen show?" Casey asked.

"Yep," Steel said, sinking into his chair and taking a deep swallow from the milk carton. "Met a woman."

"Ah, hell! You got all dolled up to watch Bodeen pick up a hooker?"

"Nope. She didn't leave with him. Her name is Megan James. Owns an antique shop just off Wilshire called Memory Lane."

"And?"

"I don't know. I'm having a check run on her. If she's in with Bodeen, she's out of her league."

"You talked to her?"

"Yeah, it . . . worked out so I could without looking conspicuous. She said her lunch date had been business."

"I'll bet. If she's not sleeping with Bodeen, then she's in it for some bucks."

"I said she wasn't sleeping with him, Casey," Steel said sharply, causing Casey to look at him in surprise.

"Yeah, fine, okay," Casey said.

"Sorry. Didn't mean to snap. What did you get today?"

"Interesting tidbit, Steel. Bodeen is feeling the pressure from all the little dealers we've busted. His network is wobbly, and he has to rebuild. In the meantime, he's after new game."

"Like what?"

"No one knows, or isn't telling. Word is, though, that Bodeen is expanding his horizons. Your guess is as good as mine. Counterfeit money? Fencing hot goods? Prostitute ring?"

"Wonderful," Steel muttered, taking another swig of milk.

"Cochise?" a man questioned, coming into the office. "You've got a real felon here in your Megan James."

"What do you mean?" Steel asked, his jaw tightening.

"Got a ticket two years ago for parking in a loading zone."

"That's it?" Steel asked, accepting the piece of paper and scanning it quickly. "Thanks."

"Any time."

"Well?" Casey asked. "Who is she?"

"Nobody, according to this. Owns Memory Lane. Lives over on Melvin. Twenty-eight. Single."

"And knows Bodeen."

"Yeah," Steel said, scowling. "She knows Frankie Bodeen."

"So whata ya think? You cover this James woman and I'll go back on the streets and see what I can dig up about Bodeen's new doings?"

"Yeah."

"Something buggin' you about this Megan James, Steel?"

Only her green eyes, long legs and full breasts, Steel thought. Only that flicker of vulnerability he'd sensed in her. Only the fact that she'd jarred him right down to his socks with her seemingly endless gazes. "No," he said. "Nothing is bothering me about Megan James."

"Okay, Pinocchio."

"Huh?"

"You're lying, Danner. I know you as well as I know myself."

"Give it a rest, Jones."

"Be careful, Steel," Casey said. "She's mixed up with Bodeen."

"Yeah, I know," he said, raking his fingers through his thick hair. "I know."

At six-thirty that evening, Megan entered her apartment and immediately tugged off her shoes. Her gaze swept over the nicely decorated room, and she ran her hand across the top of the oatmeal-colored sofa. It was her home. Hers. It would appear small to her wealthy clientele, yet to her it was a palace of splendor.

But then, she thought ruefully, heading for the bedroom, none of the patrons of Memory Lane had grown up under the same conditions as she had. The small, barren farm in Oklahoma seemed far away now, but

Megan could still recall the suffocating hopelessness she'd felt at watching her father struggling to earn a living.

Her father, whom she had loved so dearly, had raised her alone. Her mother had run off when Megan was two. When she'd graduated from high school, her father had hugged Megan tightly and urged her to leave home, to find a better place, and she had. And then six months later, he had died.

Megan stripped off her clothes and stepped into the shower, scrubbing her body with lilac-scented soap until her skin was fragrant and tingling. Then, dressed in a floor-length fluffy blue robe, she entered her yellow-toned kitchen and prepared a dinner of steak and salad. As she ate, her mind traveled back to the frightened young girl who had ridden the bus from Oklahoma to Los Angeles and gotten a job during the day as a waitress in a cheap café. At night she'd taken classes in typing and shorthand.

The business school had sent her for an interview with an elderly woman who had decided to catalog her extensive collection of antiques. Anna Turnbull had changed the course of Megan's life. Eighty, widowed and childless, Anna had seen the determination in the young girl before her, had respected the firm tilt to Megan's chin and the steady gaze she had returned unflinchingly. Anna had taken Megan under her wing and into her home.

It had been at Anna's knee that Megan had learned of the world of antiques, of their history, their wonder, their link to the past. Megan had studied with a passion, intent on making Anna proud, and on holding fast to the new woman she herself was becoming.

Megan had wept bitterly when Anna died. Wept for the loss of her friend and mentor. Wept for an era of her life that was over. In Anna's will, Megan was left five thousand dollars and a collection of twenty carefully chosen antiques. It was a legacy of love, of faith and trust that Megan could step forth and stake her claim on the life she wanted. Memory Lane was created, nurtured, grew and was hers.

"So many memories," Megan said softly. But why was it all rushing back on her today? she asked herself. Steel. Steel had looked at her with those devil eyes of his and had seen through the pretty package she had made of herself. He had gazed deep within her, and then his eyes had grown cold, harsh. Steel Danner had forced her to remember it all, and then had walked away. Would he be back?

Steel closed the door of his apartment behind him and glanced around the room. It was fairly large, nicely furnished and a total mess. Somehow, between the weekly visits from the cleaning lady, he'd managed to strew newspapers, clothes and dirty dishes from one end to the other. He shrugged out of his jacket and holster as he stepped over the debris and headed for the shower.

After showering, he dressed in faded jeans that hugged his hips and muscle-corded thighs. Then feeling hungry, he went to the kitchen and tossed a TV dinner into the oven. Having nothing better to do, he wandered into the living room where he scooped up a handful of newspapers and three socks off the sofa and dumped them on the floor.

He was a slob. Had he always been a slob? he wondered, collapsing on the sofa. No, his grandfather wouldn't have allowed it. When had he turned into a slob?

His hand slid across his bare chest and fingered the silver ornament hanging from the chain that nestled in his curly black chest hair. He cradled the object in his palm and stared at it. It was a hawk. His grandfather had begun wearing it when he had become a man, and had placed it around Steel's neck when Steel had turned fourteen. From that day forward, Steel had never taken it off.

What would become of the silver hawk when he died? Steel questioned. Would they bury it with him? He'd have no son to pass it on to. After he was gone there would be no trace that he'd ever lived.

"Hell," he said, walking back into the kitchen for a beer. "So I don't have a kid, big deal. I don't want a kid. Well, a son would be nice, or a daughter, but that would mean a wife. I sure as hell don't want a wife! Why am I talking to myself?" He was slipping over the edge in his old age.

Suddenly, he realized the direction his thoughts were leading him. No, damn it, he denied fiercely. He wasn't old. He could father twenty sons before he was through. Indian genes were heavy-duty. All his kids would look like replicas of him, even if a woman with green eyes and strawberry-blond hair gave birth to them. "What?" he said, coming to a halt. "Who? Damn you, Megan James, why are you in my head?"

After consuming his tasteless dinner and three peanut butter sandwiches, Steel was restless, edgy, totally unlike himself. He flicked the TV from station to station and finally gave it a solid whack to shut it off. Then he started to clean. He carried three bags of trash to the incinerator and stuffed the clothes hamper to overflowing. He dusted and vacuumed, loaded and ran the dishwasher, threw out strange-looking things from his refrigerator and scrubbed the bathroom and kitchen floor to within an inch of their lives.

"Not bad," he said smugly at midnight. "Let it not be said that Steel Danner is a slob!"

Tugging off his jeans and underwear, Steel slipped naked between the sheets and stared up into the darkness. He *still* wasn't tired, would never be able to sleep. He might as well work his mind since he'd run out of things for his body to do.

Bodeen, he thought. There was a nice bedtime story. Frankie Bodeen. What was Bodeen planning on getting into next? Steel and Casey had put a temporary spoke in his drug-dealing wheel, so smart Frankie was going to rebuild slow, easy, undercover. Illegal aliens? Big money in that, but it was risky, very risky. The border patrol was beefed up and ready. Frankie Bodeen and Megan James. Antiques? And do what? Rip 'em off after they'd been purchased from Memory Lane? Peanuts, penny-ante stuff. So, what was the connection between Frankie and Megan?

"Who are you, Megan James?" Steel said to the night. "Just who in the hell are you?"

Steel never dreamed. When he slept, he slept, rejuvenating his body and blanking his mind. But that night he dreamed. In strange, twisting pictures he saw Frankie, who was laughing, and Roddy and Brian, who stared only into each other's eyes and paid no attention to Steel. And then he saw Megan, who reached out her hand and accepted from Steel the silver hawk, which she placed on her stomach, pressing it there before putting the chain over her head, the hawk coming to rest between her breasts.

Steel woke, drenched in sweat. He stared into the darkness until the first rays of dawn crept across the room.

Three

___

Steel dressed in black jeans and a burgundy-colored sweater, then zipped a lightweight gray windbreaker halfway up to conceal his revolver. His head hurt. It pounded as though he'd gotten blitzed the night before. Apparently, cleaning didn't agree with his nervous system, he thought. He was in a helluva lousy mood.

Just as he headed for the door, the telephone rang.

"Danner," he said into the receiver, squeezing his aching forehead with his fingers.

"Steel? It's Casey. Ready for this? The Feds got a tip that Bodeen was in Paris two months ago."

"What in the hell for?" Steel snapped. "Oh-h-h, my head."

"How should I know, Mr. Sunshine. You hung over?"

"No, I'm not hung over, Julian!"

"Julian! You're dead meat, Pocahontas! What is your problem, Steel?"

"Sorry, Casey. I've got a rotten headache."

"Did you take some aspirin?"

"No."

"Gosh, you're smart. Take two aspirin, flea brain."

"Good idea. I think I will. The Feds have no clue as to why Bodeen went to Paris?"

"Nope. They're still digging, though."

"Hell."

"True. I'm hitting the streets. You?"

"I'm going to watch the traffic going in and out of Megan James's store, then drop in later and pay a social call."

"Enjoy. Don't forget to take your aspirin."

"Yeah. See ya."

A thorough search of the cupboards produced no aspirin, and Steel headed out the door with a deep scowl on his face. He stopped at a drugstore, purchased a newspaper, a metal tin of aspirin and a Styrofoam cup of milk, then settled on a bench in the park across the street from Memory Lane. And then he waited.

A half hour later, Megan walked across the park, the morning breeze fluffing her hair around her cheeks and lifting the skirt of her blue linen dress engagingly above her knees. She laughed softly and brushed down her skirt as she tossed her head to flick back her hair. In front of the fountain, she stopped and reached into her purse for the small coin bag containing her pennies. After dropping the coin in the water, she ran her hand through the spray, then continued on her way.

Steel let out a long breath and only then realized he'd been hardly breathing during the scenario he'd witnessed. Megan was a vision of loveliness, he thought.

She had looked happy, carefree, young and beautiful. Very, very beautiful. He'd had a glimpse of her shapely legs as the wind whipped her skirt above her knees, and his heart had pounded as loudly as the ache in his head. What had she wished for today with her coin in the fountain?

Steel jerked his wrists and snapped the paper in front of him, reading the baseball scores for the sixth time. Did Megan know that Bodeen had been in Paris? he wondered. What in the hell was in Paris? Every time he tried to figure it out, his head pounded. He never had headaches, but this one was a doozy. His grandfather would have whipped up some foul-smelling concoction out of herbs and junk that would have fixed him up. Did Megan know Bodeen had been in Paris? Ah, hell, his head hurt!

His grandfather, Steel fumed almost two hours later, had failed to mention that the Indian trick of separating one's mind from the here and now did not work when a man had a headache! He'd had it! He wasn't going to wait another minute. There was no smog, the sun was beating down on him and he couldn't take off his jacket because he was wearing his revolver. The traffic in and out of Megan's had been steady. Boring, but steady.

Steel checked his watch. Eleven-thirty. Close enough to lunch. It was time to visit Memory Lane.

He tossed the cup and newspaper in the trash barrel and walked across the park, his gaze lingering for a moment on the fountain and the coins shimmering on the bottom beneath the rippling water. Secrets of the heart, he thought. That's what Megan had said. Wishes in a fountain were secrets of the heart.

Steel stopped and raised his large hand, resting it on his chest so he could feel the silver hawk beneath his sweater. A son, he thought. A son to pass the silver hawk on to. A son to wear the name Danner, to walk tall, proud of his Indian heritage. A blend of Steel and the woman who had carried the child in her womb. A new life, an extension of Blade of Steel and his lady. Yeah, a son.

Steel pulled a coin from his pocket and stared at it for a moment. This was crazy! he thought, shaking his head. Why was he so hell-bent on having a son all of a sudden? He'd never given it one minute's thought before except to know that the hearth and home bit was not for him. But now it was on his mind constantly.

"Ah, hell," he said, and tossed the coin into the water, then went into the shop.

Megan stood behind the counter and raised her eyes as the door opened and the man entered. Steel! Oh, thank God, he was there! she thought wildly. He'd come back!

Ah, man, look at her, Steel thought. She was so lovely, fragile, exquisite. He needed to hold this woman, feel her soft lips move under his. He needed to pull her to him, mold her against him and touch and caress every inch of her slender body. Megan.

Steel walked slowly forward as Megan came from behind the counter and met him in the middle of the room, staring up at him with her large green eyes. Neither one of them spoke nor hardly seemed to breathe. Of their own volition it seemed, Steel's large hands lifted to cup Megan's face, his thumbs trailing over the soft skin of her cheeks.

The warmth from Steel's hands brought a flush to Megan's cheeks, then the heat traveled throughout her, causing a trembling within. The store disappeared into a hazy mist. Time lost meaning as they stood there, filling their senses with the sight and aroma of each other.

"Steel?" Megan finally whispered.

"You knew I'd be back didn't you?" he asked, smiling slightly as he slowly pulled his hands away.

"No. Yes. I don't know," she said, taking a step backward as she pressed her hands to her burning cheeks. "I don't understand what just happened or... Go away, Steel. Oh, please, go and leave me alone!"

"Megan, no!" he murmured, reaching out and gripping her by the upper arms. "No way. Something is taking place between us that we can't ignore. Don't shut me out. Don't be afraid of me, or try to fight what's happening between us. Look, let's go to lunch, okay?"

"No!"

"Yes! We'll talk, just chat. I won't touch you. We'll be two people having lunch and—"

"Hello," someone said as the door opened.

"Clara!" Megan said as Steel released her arms. "There you are! Right on time to take over."

"I've never been late," Clara said, looking at Megan, then Steel. "Is something wrong?"

"Wrong? No, of course not," Megan said. "I'm going to lunch. I'll get my purse."

Steel smiled at Clara, who eyed him warily as Megan hurried into her office. Something about Clara seemed strange, slightly off. Steel couldn't quite figure out why, but she immediately aroused his suspicions.

"Worked here long?" he asked pleasantly.

"Couple months," she said. "Are you a friend of Megan's or a client?"

"Friend."

"I thought so. You aren't the antique type."

"No?"

"No-o-o," she said slowly, her eyes shifting over him.

Streetwise, Steel thought. This kid was definitely streetwise. Clara had been around the block a few times. "Well, I'll tell you, Clara," he said, looking at her steadily, "you're not exactly the antique type, either."

"It's a living," she shrugged, then stomped behind the counter, the discussion over for the time being.

Megan applied lip gloss with a trembling hand and then stared at her reflection in the mirror. Her eyes were bright, too bright, and her skin was flushed.

Oh, dear heaven, what had happened? Never had she been so glad to see someone as she'd been when Steel walked in the door. They hadn't even spoken; they had just moved toward one another as naturally as breathing. Steel was so strong yet so gentle, and she'd felt so safe, protected, when he'd cradled her face in his hands. Nothing had mattered but Steel; his touch, his special male aroma, everything. It felt so right that it must be wrong. Everything was moving so quickly. And now they were going to lunch. Lunch. Yes. Good. Public place, normal conversation, and things would get back into perspective.

"Ready?" Steel said, when Megan returned to the front of the store.

"Yes."

"See ya, Clara," Steel said, winking at the girl.

"Goodbye . . . sir," Clara said sullenly.

"Clara?" Megan said, turning to look at her questioningly.

"Have a nice time," Clara said, smiling sweetly.

"I won't be long," Megan said.

"Yes, she will," Steel said, opening the door. "Don't wait up."

Out on the sidewalk, Megan frowned. "You shouldn't have said that," she said. "Clara might think . . . well, I mean—"

"Don't worry about it. You're the boss, remember? Feel like walking? There's a café a couple blocks down."

"Fine. It's a lovely day. Aren't you warm in that jacket?"

"No, I'm fine," he said, shoving his hands into his pockets. He was roasting. But he knew he couldn't exactly take the jacket off and stroll along with a shoulder holster as decoration. He was also going to keep his hands in his pockets and off Megan James! He'd never done anything so cornball in his life. Walk into a woman's business, touch her, stare into her eyes, without even saying hello? But, damn, he hadn't been able to stop himself.

"You seem to set your own hours," Megan said pleasantly. "Are you on vacation?"

"No, I'm . . . in investments. I have a company with my brother-in-law."

"Is it interesting work?"

"Sometimes," he said, opening the door to the restaurant. He had to lie to her, he knew that, but it caused a knot to tighten in his stomach. Hell, what was *he* getting the guilts about? he thought. *She* was the one who was mixed up with Frankie Bodeen.

They were led to a cozy circular booth in the corner that had a candle flickering in the center of the table. After they had ordered, Steel spread his long arms out across the top of the puffed leather seat and looked at

Megan. If he raised his hand, he could weave it through her silky hair, and the very thought caused him to tighten his grip on the booth.

"Tell me about the antique business," he said. "Where do you find all that old stuff?"

"Different ways. Auctions, estates, people needing ready cash."

"Do you ever go out of the country to collect things?" he asked. Like Paris, for example? What in the hell was in Paris?

"Occasionally, when there's something very special one of my clients wants. Usually, I can find plenty of merchandise here, although I do travel up and down the coast for auctions."

"Interesting. Okay, so you have all these ways of keeping your store supplied, but suppose you don't have what I want?"

"Well, I'd do a search, try to locate your item and see if and when it's going to be auctioned. You tell me how much you're willing to pay, and I go in and bid to your limit. You, of course, are paying for my services."

"Of course," Steel said, smiling. "What about a megabucks boy like the man you had lunch with yesterday?" Easy, Danner, he thought. Nice and easy. "Now, he obviously doesn't need to sell anything to pay the rent, so did he put you hot on the trail of something he's after?" If she tensed, he'd drop it for now, wouldn't push it.

"Oh, you mean Mr. Sands?"

"Whoever he was," Steel said, shrugging his shoulders.

"His name is Frank Sands. He wants a very special gift for his wife, but hasn't decided exactly what it should be. He said he'd get back to me, but who knows?

I got a fancy lunch out of it, and I also made a complete fool of myself staring at you across the room."

"Well, I stared at you, too, so we're even," he said, smiling at her. Frank Sands, he thought. And he'd decide what he wanted and get back to her? Was Megan blowing smoke? No, damn it, she was telling the truth! She had to be because he needed this woman to be everything she appeared to be on the surface. She was soft, warm, feminine, sensuous and had an underlying vulnerability. She was . . . Megan.

"Steel," Megan said softly, "where do you go when your eyes become so cold? Even in the candlelight I can see the change."

"I'm here, Megan," he said, giving up the struggle with himself and sifting her hair through his fingers.

"Not always, Steel."

Before Steel could think of a reply, the waitress arrived with their meal, and they spent the next several minutes in silence as they took the sharp edge off their appetites.

"Do you have an ulcer?" Megan asked suddenly.

"Me? No. Why?"

"Because yesterday and today you ordered coffee *and* a glass of milk. I thought perhaps you had stomach problems."

"Nope. I just happen to like milk. You're very observant."

"Maybe I should be a detective," she said, smiling.

"Yeah," he said, frowning. "They probably always need more cops on the force."

"I suppose."

"Are you originally from L.A.?"

"Yes," she said. And a farm across the country where there were no hopes or dreams. "Are you?"

"No, I grew up in northern Arizona on the Hopi reservation, went to Arizona State University outside of Phoenix, then settled here later." As he talked, Steel absently ran his fingers across his forehead. The ache behind his temples was still throbbing.

"Do you have a headache?" Megan asked. "You've rubbed your forehead about six times."

"Yeah, I woke up with it, and I guess it's here for the day. Must have slept wrong."

"Have you taken something for it?"

"Yes, some aspirin," he said, taking the tin out of his jacket pocket and flipping it open. "In fact, a whole bunch," he added, setting the empty container on the table.

"You took all of those?"

"Apparently so. I just kept popping them in and didn't realize that I'd nearly OD'd."

Megan cocked her head and frowned as she studied his face. "Your eyes are soupy," she said.

"Soupy?" he said, laughing. "Cold, warm, now soupy? You've really got this thing for analyzing my eyes."

"I mean it. I think you have a fever," she said, placing her hand on his forehead.

"Nice, cool," he said, bringing her hand to his mouth and kissing the palm. "You have pretty hands, Megan."

A tingling sensation swept from Megan's hand, where Steel's lips had rested, traveled up her arm and then across her breasts. She felt her breasts grow taut beneath her dress; they ached, needed, wanted to be touched by Steel's strong but gentle hands.

"Steel," she said, slowly withdrawing her hand from his, "I'm sure you have a fever. Are you coughing? Ache all over? Chest hurt?"

"None of the above. Are you a closet Florence Nightingale?"

"No, it's probably my mothering instincts coming to the surface."

"Do you hope to be a mother someday?" he asked. His dream, he thought. The silver hawk. His coin in the fountain. Now he was even *talking* about babies!

"Yes, I'd like to have a child."

"And a husband?"

"It usually goes hand in hand."

"Not in these liberated times. A lot of women decide to have kids and raise them alone."

"I wouldn't. I want to be a part of an old-fashioned unit. Mother, father, baby, dog, cat and a goldfish."

"A goldfish?" Steel said, smiling in delight. "That's a mandatory part of your scenario?"

"Absolutely. There must be a goldfish in a pretty bowl with marbles on the bottom."

"Is that what you wish for when you throw your coin in the fountain? A husband, baby, goldfish?"

"No," she said quietly, "that's not what I wish for. I should be getting back to the store."

"Clara's there."

"I know, but some of the customers prefer to deal only with me and I spoil them rotten and cater to their wishes."

"How'd you happen to hire Clara?" he said casually, before draining his coffee cup.

"She just showed up looking for work. She bounced in so full of enthusiasm and said, 'Hi, I'm Clara Bodeen,' and I..."

A roaring noise echoed in Steel's ears and momentarily blocked out Megan's words. That was Clara Bodeen at Memory Lane? he asked himself. What was Frankie Bodeen up to?

"...and she's an excellent worker," Megan was saying. "She can do absolutely everything. The clasp broke on my bracelet one day, and Clara fixed it for me. Then the coffeepot just suddenly quit working, so she dismantled it, found the problem and put it all back together. She's a gem."

"How long has Clara been at Memory Lane?" Steel asked. Man, Megan was a one-woman fan club of Clara's. Was Megan so gullible that she couldn't see what a tough cookie Clara was? Or was Megan deliberately trying to give the impression that Clara was Miss Wonderful?

"Clara's been with me just over two months. I really must get back, Steel."

"Yeah, okay. Megan, would you have dinner with me tonight?"

"I..."

"How about pizza and beer? I'm really in the mood for pizza and beer. Wear jeans. Seven o'clock?"

"I don't know, Steel."

"Don't be frightened of me, Megan. Even more, don't be afraid of whatever it is that's happening between us. We'll just take it slow and easy. Seven?"

"Yes, all right. It's been ages since I've had pizza and beer. It sounds like fun. Here, I'll write down my address."

Which he'd already memorized, Steel thought. This was smooth. He was picking up more and more information through idle conversation with Megan. They'd chat over dinner. But ah, hell, who was he kidding? He wanted to be with her tonight as a man, not a cop. Never before in his career had he gotten emotionally or physically involved with a woman tangled up in one of his cases. Until now. No wonder he had a headache. His brain was dissolving. What he was doing with Megan was not smart. Not smart at all.

Steel and Megan were silent as they strolled back to the shop. In front of Memory Lane, Steel shoved his hands into his jacket pockets again. "I'll see you at seven," he said.

"All right. Thank you for lunch. I hope your headache goes away."

"Yeah, me too. See ya. I..." Damn, he needed to kiss her! He *had* to kiss her!

Their eyes met for a long moment, then slowly, slowly, he lowered his head and claimed her mouth with his. Softly, sensuously, Steel brushed his lips over Megan's with a touch as soft as a butterfly's wing. Then, with a throaty moan, he gathered her into his arms, and she circled his neck with her hands as the kiss intensified.

The pressure of her hands increased to bring him closer, closer, to receive his lips, his tongue, his heat, his strength. Her tongue flickered against his, and she felt him tense as their mouths moved together with feverish urgency.

Time, space, reality and reason were swept into oblivion and replaced by euphoria as heartbeats raced and breathing became labored. Passions soared. And the kiss went on and on.

Steel filled his senses with the feel of Megan, the taste, the aroma. Blood pounded through his veins, and his manhood stirred, straining against the tight fabric of his jeans. A small voice crept into his consciousness, then grew louder, screaming at him to stop before it was too late. But, oh, God, how he wanted this woman! Never

before had he desired anyone the way he did Megan
James. But he had to stop!

"Megan!" he gasped, taking a ragged breath as he
pulled her hands from his neck.

"Steel?" she whispered, her lips swollen, her emerald eyes smoky with desire as she gazed up at him, appearing slightly confused.

"Your little old ladies will go into cardiac arrest," he
said, his voice hoarse as he moved her gently away from
him.

"Oh, Steel, I . . ."

"Tonight," he said, trailing his thumb over her
cheek, before turning and striding away.

"Bye, Steel," she said softly, watching until he disappeared from view. A gentle expression was on her
face as she walked slowly into the store.

For the remainder of the afternoon Megan smiled.
She felt absolutely, positively wonderful. Steel Danner
made her feel feminine and pretty, and in a few hours
she would be with him again. Megan James was in a
terrific mood.

Steel Danner was not in a good mood.

"Hi, Cochise," an officer said, as Steel strode into
the police station.

"I want a check on Clara Bodeen."

"When? Pronto, Tonto?"

"Now," Steel said, rapping his knuckles on the
counter. "Right now."

"You've got it, Chief Clench His Jaw. I don't mess
with you when you're in this mood."

"Good," Steel growled, stalking out the door.

"Circle the wagons!" the man yelled. "Blade of Steel
is on the warpath again!"

"Ginger," Steel said, stopping at a desk, "do you have any aspirin?"

"Well, darn it, Steel, when are you going to ask me for my body? Last week it was a pencil, now it's aspirin. I swear I dieted until I was faint with hunger, and do you ask for my body? No! All you want are pencils and—"

"Ginger!"

"Two aspirin, coming right up," the pretty blonde said. "No fuss, no muss. You've got that mean glint in your eyes today, Sitting Bull."

"Damn it! What is it all of a sudden about my eyes?" Steel roared. "Give me the damn pills!"

"Here!" Ginger said, dropping them into his hand. "I withdraw the offer of my body."

"Cripe," Steel muttered, heading down the hall. "Everyone around here is a loony tune."

The office was empty when Steel entered, and he downed his aspirin with the milk he'd retrieved from the kitchen. After removing his jacket and holster, he sank into his chair, propped his feet on the desk and leaned his head back, closing his eyes. Five minutes later he was asleep.

The next sensation Steel registered was a gentle thud against his chest, then another. He opened his eyes, peered down and saw a wad of paper ricochet off of his sweater.

"Target practice?" he asked, looking across the room at Casey.

"Hey, the last time I shook you to wake you up I was pinned against the wall with your arm crushing my Adam's apple. This is much safer. How's life?"

"Don't ask."

"How's your head?"

"Don't ask."

"There's nothing on the streets about Bodeen's plans," Casey said. "Zip. How'd you do?"

"Is he awake?" a man said, poking his head in the door.

"Enter," Casey said, waving the man in.

"Here's your rundown, Steel. More interesting than yesterday's."

"Thanks. I appreciate this," Steel said. "You're not only an officer, but a gentleman. Your mother must be proud of you."

"Go back to sleep, Cochise. You're not a well man. Bye, guys."

"This department hires strange people, Casey," Steel said. "Okay, let's see here."

"What's up?"

"Clara *Bodeen* has worked at Megan James's antique store, for almost three months."

"Clara Bodeen?"

"Yeah." Steel quickly read over the report, then dropped it on his desk. "Ho-ho, right on the money. Clara Bodeen is Frankie's niece and has a rap sheet as long as your arm for two-bit drug dealing."

"And where does Megan James fit into all of this, Steel?"

"She doesn't, Casey. I think Bodeen's setting Megan up for something. He puts his niece in to check out the operation on a daily basis and to get a clear picture of how Memory Lane is run."

"But what's going down?"

"That, my friend, I don't know. Bodeen approached Megan as Frank Sands, who wants an antique for his wife and is deciding what Megan should get him."

"And Megan?"

"She's clean, Casey."

"How can you be so sure?"

"I just know."

"Damn it, Steel, that's not good enough! You've gone and done it, haven't you? You're involved with this James woman, and now you've decided she's as pure as the driven snow. You've *never* done anything like this. What in the hell is the matter with you, man?"

Steel slammed the desk with his fist, and in the next instant was on his feet, his dark eyes flashing with anger. "Damn you, Casey! You've always trusted my gut instincts before!"

"I know, buddy," Casey said quietly, "but this time I think the instincts are coming from your heart."

Four

Steel stiffened, and every muscle in his body tensed as he stared at Casey Jones. After drawing a deep breath and looking at the ceiling for a long moment to control his raging anger, Steel walked to the window. Shoving his hands into his back pockets, palms out, he stood rigid, shoulders taut and straight.

"Where is Megan from?" Casey asked.

"Here. L.A.," Steel said, his voice flat, low.

"Have you checked it out? Family background? Who her people are? Schooling? Where she got the money for the antique store?"

"No."

"Don't you think you should?"

"Yeah."

"Steel, what are you going to do if Megan is in this thing with Bodeen?"

"I'll arrest her," he grated, a muscle twitching in the strong column of his neck.

"Do you want off the case?"

"No!" Steel said, spinning around. "Damn," he said, reaching out his hand to grip the back of the chair.

"What's wrong?" Casey asked, getting quickly to his feet and coming around the desk.

"Room is going around."

"Here, sit," Casey said, easing Steel into the chair. "Hell, man, you're burning up with fever. You're sick, Steel."

"I never get sick."

"Guess again. You're out on your feet. Indians are tough dudes, but you're not immune to illness. Go home and get some rest. Everything will keep for another day."

"I—"

"Casey, Steel," a man said, poking his head in the door, "Captain wants you in his office."

"Tell him I died," Steel growled.

"Now, hotshots! The boys from the Bureau are here."

"That's all I need," Steel said. "The suit-and-tie guys with the preppy haircuts."

"Let's get this over with," Casey said, "then you can go home to bed. Your decadent life is catching up with you, Steel. You're all worn out."

"Stow it," Steel grumbled, pushing himself to his feet. He followed Casey out the door and toward the captain's office.

Captain Meredith waved the two men into the room and introduced them to Agents Townes and Mendoza from the Federal Bureau of Investigation. As the others sat down, Steel leaned his shoulder against the wall and crossed his arms over his chest. He definitely was not smiling.

"Lieutenant Danner, Lieutenant Jones," Agent Townes said, "we've received a tip that Frankie Bodeen was in Paris."

"Gosh," Casey said, "you guys are amazing. What else is new?"

Steel's laughter, which he attempted to stifle, came out in the form of a snort, and Captain Meredith glared at his two lieutenants.

"So, what's in Paris?" Steel inquired.

"Could be anything," Townes said, "but we're ruling out drugs. You two have broken his drug ring and he'll have to regroup. There's no sense in him bringing in a big shipment when he doesn't have the people to move it on the streets. Bodeen must be after your butts."

"Nope," Casey said, "it's been handled with finesse for eight months. Steel and I did all the work and gave the collars to the uniforms. It just looks like a bunch of cops got lucky. Bodeen would have sent his muscle after me and Steel by now if he'd made the connection."

"Nice," Mendoza said, nodding.

"How can you stand those neckties all day?" Steel asked, and was awarded with another stormy glare by Captain Meredith.

"So?" Casey said. "Why was Frankie in Paris?"

"Artwork, maybe," Townes said. "Jewels. Negotiable bonds. Your guess is as good as mine. It wasn't a pleasure trip, though. We figure he's working up to smuggling something in."

"Now hold it," Steel said, raising his hand. "That's international and in your jurisdiction. Are you saying you're taking over our—"

"No," Mendoza said.

"Cancel the war dance," Casey muttered.

"We're extending your jurisdiction for this case," Mendoza said. "You know Bodeen better than I know my brother. We'll document it and dump it back in your lap. The minute our man picks up any more info on Bodeen's jaunt to Paris, he'll report directly to you."

"How very magnanimous of you, my dear," Casey said.

"Can it," Captain Meredith said. "Fake it. Show some couth."

"Do the Feds pay for your neckties?" Steel said.

"Danner!" the captain said.

"I want to know if my taxes are going for those ties!" Steel protested.

"Oh, man," Casey said laughing.

"Listen up, you yo-yos," Captain Meredith said. "Bodeen could be into anything and everything. Whatever it is, he'll need a place to move it. Any leads?"

"We're checking something out," Steel said quietly.

"Okay," the captain sighed, "it's all yours. Get out of here and earn your money."

"Great talking to you," Casey said, nodding to the agents. "I swear, you boys just dress so damn spiffy, ya know what I mean?"

"Out!" Captain Meredith yelled as Steel and Casey left the room.

Back in the office, Steel pulled on his shoulder holster and jacket.

"It's adding up, Steel," Casey said. "Bodeen is bringing in something artsy-craftsy that can be shuffled through an antique store."

"Yep."

"You going home?"

"Nope."

"You're sick, Steel!"

"You said it yourself. I haven't checked out Megan's background. I'll do it, show you she's clean and that's it."

"Get some rest first."

"No! I should have automatically followed up when she said she had lived here all her life. I'm taking care of it right now."

"Steel, in all the years I've known you, I've never seen you lose it over a woman. You're setting yourself up to be ripped to shreds if this goes bad about Megan."

"I'll live," he said, striding to the door.

"Will you, Steel?" Casey said to the empty room.

A long, frustrating three hours later, Steel let himself into his apartment and collapsed on the sofa. Nothing. Absolutely nothing. Megan James had not been born in Los Angeles. There was no record of her even existing until she applied for the business license to open Memory Lane. A bank loan application, which Steel had flashed his badge to see, showed her as a native of California, single, no family and having a degree from UCLA. Megan James had never been registered as a student at UCLA. She'd lied.

Steel ran his hand down his face, feeling the unhealthy heat of his skin and shivered as a chill swept through him. His head pounded with an increasingly painful cadence, and he felt as though he had a brick on his chest. As each search turned up nothing on Megan, a knot tightened in his stomach and stayed there, twisting his insides. He had waited for the anger to consume him, but it never came. He was registering no emotion whatsoever. Nothing. He felt empty, drained, numb.

Pushing himself to his feet, Steel waited for the dizziness that assaulted him to pass, then with slow steps headed for the shower.

In her bedroom, Megan hummed softly as she blow-dried her freshly shampooed hair, then dressed in designer jeans and a green sweater that matched her eyes perfectly. She pushed her feet into loafers, then sprayed a light perfume across her throat. Her hair was a shining cascade of soft waves and her eyes were clear and sparkling.

At seven o'clock, Blade of Steel Danner knocked on her door.

"Hello, Steel," Megan said, smiling. "Come in."

"Thanks," he said, his trained eyes immediately assessing the furnishings of the apartment before returning to Megan and her slender figure outlined in casual clothes. "You look nice. I like you dressed like that."

"You don't approve of the attire I wear for my clients?" she said, laughing as she drank in the sight of him in tight jeans and a black sweater. He hadn't smiled, not once, she thought. He hadn't kissed, or even touched her. His eyes were cloudy, unreadable, and there was a tension emanating from his rugged length. Oh, dear heaven, what was wrong? "Would you like something? Wine? Scotch?"

"Scotch, please. Neat."

"I'll get it. Please, sit down."

Steel sat on the sofa and rested his elbows on his knees, making a steeple of his fingers as he stared unseeing across the room. Megan had lied, he thought fiercely. She hadn't been born in L.A. It was as though she'd dropped out of the heavens into Memory Lane. He had wanted to haul her into his arms and kiss her when he'd come in. He'd also wanted to shake her until her teeth rattled and demand she tell him the truth. Instead, he'd done nothing. He'd asked for a drink and sat down on her plushy sofa like a casual date.

Steel sighed and slouched lower, leaning his head against the back of the sofa and shutting his eyes. Man, he felt lousy, he thought. Every bone in his body ached. He was hot one minute, freezing the next. If he had had half a brain he'd have stayed home in bed, but he'd have only lain there going over and over it in his mind. Who in the hell was Megan James?

"Steel?" Megan asked.

"What?" he asked, pushing himself to an upright position. "Oh, thanks," he said, accepting the drink, his fingers brushing against Megan's.

"Your hand is hot," she said, sitting down next to him and placing her palm on his forehead. "Steel, you're burning up."

"I'm okay," he said, downing the Scotch in one swallow and gasping as it burned his throat.

"You're very sick!"

"Let's go eat."

"Absolutely not! You should be in bed."

"Is that an offer?" he said, smiling at her rather crookedly. Damn, the room was spinning like a top, he thought foggily. Megan was saying something because her lips were moving, but he couldn't quite hear her. Noise, roaring noise, was blaring in his ears.

"Up," Megan said, pulling on his arm.

"Huh?"

"Get up, Steel."

"I'm up. Aren't I?"

"No, come on. That's it, lean on me, put one foot in front of the other."

"Where am I going? Oh, yeah, pizza."

"Goodness, you're heavy. Just a little further. There. Now sit down on the bed."

"Bed?" he said, shaking his head. He couldn't think! Nothing was making sense! he thought. Damn!

Megan pushed Steel back against the pillow and then lifted his legs onto the bed. He sighed deeply and closed his eyes.

"Steel?" she asked, leaning over and peering at his flushed face. "Are you in there? Nope. This is cute." Now what will I do with him? she wondered. He's got a fever. Sponge baths. Yes! Well! Take off his clothes. Oh, dear heaven.

Megan tugged off Steel's shoes and socks and dropped them on the floor. Then she pushed and pulled the heavy inert man until she managed to remove his sweater. Her breath caught in her throat as she saw his glistening torso. His skin was dripping with sweat, the corded muscles gleaming beneath the curly mass of dark, damp hair on his chest. She lifted the silver hawk and rested it in the palm of her hand, brushing her fingertip over the smooth surface before laying it carefully back in place.

Magnificent, she thought, her eyes roaming over Steel's chest, shoulders and arms. Like a sculpted statue, bronzed to perfection. And now she had to take off his pants! She was going to faint dead out on the floor!

Megan undid the belt on Steel's jeans, then slid down the zipper. Inch by inch, she worked the fabric over his hips, thighs, along his legs, averting her eyes from his dark-blue underwear and his well-defined sexuality beneath. Steel moaned and moved his head on the pillow, but didn't open his eyes.

Megan's heart raced as she viewed the sleeping man. He was beautiful. He was masculinity personified, a bold announcement of the differences between man and woman. He was power, and strength, and steely muscles. He was also sick as a dog.

When Megan scooped up Steel's clothes to put them on a chair, a flat black folder fell out of the back pocket of his jeans. As she picked it up, it opened in her hand and she stared at it in disbelief, her trembling legs forcing her to drop into the chair.

Steel Danner was a detective with the Los Angeles Police Department!

A cacophony of voices screamed in Megan's mind. Steel was a detective, a police officer! He had lied to her, said he worked in investments. Why? Why had he lied? It hurt. The thought of Steel lying to her hurt so much. And it was frightening. What did he want from her? Why had he suddenly appeared in her life? She hadn't done anything wrong! She was an ordinary citizen, running an ordinary business.

"Pizza," Steel mumbled. "Megan. Hot. So damn hot."

Megan jumped to her feet, shoved the leather case back into the pocket of the jeans, then folded Steel's clothes and placed them on the chair. In the bathroom, she filled a basin with tepid water and returned to the edge of the bed with the container and a washcloth.

For the next hour, she made endless trips back and forth as the water became too cool. She sponged Steel's body from head to toe, over and over. She blanked her mind, refusing to pay credence to the fingers of desire that traveled throughout her as she worked, refusing to hear the questions pounding in her mind about Blade of Steel Danner.

Steel moved his head restlessly on the pillow several times, then would settle back into a heavy sleep, his breathing raspy in the quiet room. He spoke often, but Megan could not comprehend what he was saying. As she once again wrung out the washcloth, Steel said one word with crystal clarity.

"Bodeen."

Megan's hands stopped in midair, and her eyes widened as she stared at Steel's face. Bodeen? she thought. Clara? Clara Bodeen? Her name had come up at lunch, but why would Steel's mind be centering on Megan's clerk? Oh, this didn't make sense!

"Ah, hell," Steel said, his dark lashes fluttering against his cheeks and lifting slowly to reveal cloudy eyes. "What—where—"

"Shhh," Megan said. "You're ill and I'm taking care of you."

"Megan?" he said, his voice thick.

"Yes, Steel, it's me. Just lie quietly. Here, I'll cover you over so you don't get a chill."

"My clothes!"

"It's all right. I have them."

"Where's my gun? Where in the hell is my gun?"

"You didn't bring it, remember? It's probably in your car."

"Yeah, yeah, right," he said, shutting his eyes. "Okay."

"Lieutenant Danner?" Megan said softly.

"Yeah?"

"Nothing," she said, tears prickling the back of her eyes. "I just wondered if that's who you really are. Rest, Lieutenant Blade of Steel."

"Mmmm."

Twice during the next hour, Megan roused Steel enough to get him to drink some orange juice. His breathing was not as labored, but his skin was still much too hot beneath her cool hand. His mumblings had ceased, and he began to rest easier, appearing relaxed. Yet even in slumber there was power, strength, emanating from his body, and Megan wrapped her arms around her elbows in a protective gesture as she stared down at him.

How complacent her life had been until she had sat in the restaurant, raised her eyes, and seen him, she thought. Steel evoked hidden passions within her and brought a smile to her lips that was real. Steel made her heart race and her senses soar. He made her feel infinitely glad she was a woman. She was stirred within by his touch and feel and aroma, and by the changing moods reflected in his fathomless dark eyes.

He was Blade of Steel Danner.

And he had lied.

Megan suddenly felt exhausted, drained, robbed of her last ounce of energy. She wanted only to sleep, to escape from the maze in her mind, the endless questions, the fear, and the pain of Steel's deception.

Megan shut off the lights in the living room, locked the door and walked slowly back into the bedroom. She would stay with Steel in case he needed her in the night. He was sleeping on top of the bedspread covered in a blanket, so she would crawl between the sheets. Safe enough. Not that a sick man who was dead to the world was much of a threat, she thought ruefully.

She changed into a faded football jersey and turned off the light before getting into bed. Moonlight flickered across the bed, casting an eerie luminescence over the expanse. Propping herself up on her elbow, she gazed at Steel. She wanted to lay her head on his chest, hear the steady beat of his heart. She wanted him to lift his dark lashes and reveal eyes free of fever—eyes gentle, warm, loving. She wanted him to lower his mouth to hers and sweep her away into oblivion. And she wanted him to make love to her, to bring to her the promise of his masculinity, to consume her, fill her, claim her as his.

Claim her as his? she thought. Just in body, or did she mean more? Was she falling in love with Blade of Steel Danner? It was as though he were already intricately woven into her life, her mind, her heart. Were the tempestuous emotions he evoked within her leading to love? "Oh, God, no!" she whispered, sinking back against her pillow.

With a groan, Megan rolled onto her stomach, rearranged her pillow into a ball and fell into an exhausted, dreamless sleep.

A yellowy cast from dawn's light replaced the silvery glow of the moon and woke Megan. She blinked, yawned, then snapped her mouth closed as the events of the previous night hammered into her consciousness. Turning her head, she saw Steel sleeping peacefully, the stubby growth of beard on his face making his skin appear even darker.

Megan pushed back the blanket and rolled over to peer at Steel's face. She raised her hand to place it on his forehead to check his fever and resisted the urge to trace her fingertips over his sensuous lips.

The instant her palm came to rest on Steel's forehead, a scream erupted from Megan's lips as viselike fingers circled her neck and she was flung backward, instantly pinned beneath the crushing weight of Steel's body.

"What in the hell—Megan?" he said, shaking his head as if clearing it of a foggy haze.

"You're...choking...me!" she gasped.

"What? Lord, I'm sorry," he said, jerking his hand from her throat.

"You're smashing me flat!"

"Oh," he said, shifting off her, but keeping her partially covered and pinned firmly in place by his scantily clothed body. "What's going on here? That's sunlight. What happened to last night? Where are my clothes? Why are we in this bed together?"

"Anything else?" Megan said, frowning. "Get off me!"

"No. Not until I get some answers."

"You're breaking every bone in my body!"

"I am not! Talk to me!"

"You were sick, remember? You nearly passed out on your face, so I put you to bed and sponged you down because I could have fried an egg on your head. A lot of thanks I get! You nearly strangle me and now you're crushing me to smithereens."

"You slipped something in my drink," Steel said, squinting at her.

"Oh, shut up. You're so stupid you didn't have enough sense to stay home in bed where you belonged. So what happens? I get stuck with you. I should have shoved you out the door."

A slow smile tugged at the corners of Steel's mouth and widened into a grin. "That's a helluva temper you've got there, lady," he said. "Your hair is more red than I realized. There are laser beams shooting from those gorgeous green eyes of yours."

"Move it!"

"No, no, I have to collect my data here. Yes, I felt lousy when I arrived. Check. Then I had a drink. Check. Then the rest is a blur. You sponged me down because I had a fever?"

"Yes."

"Tsk, tsk, and to think I missed all that tender, loving care."

"Damn it, Steel, I'm going to—"

"Uh-oh, now she's swearing. What would the Memory Lane old ladies think?"

"Would you stop?" she demanded, bursting into laughter. "This is ridiculous. How do you feel?"

"You tell me, Megan," he said softly, slowly lowering his mouth to hers. "Tell me . . . how this . . . feels."

It was ecstasy.

Their lips met hungrily, eagerly, and Megan welcomed Steel's tongue into the hidden darkness of her mouth. His tongue delved and dipped, drew circles around her own flickering tongue and sent shock waves of desire spiraling throughout her. Steel's hand slid down her side and up again beneath the material of her jersey to gently grasp her breast, his thumb stroking the nipple into a taut bud. Megan moaned deep in her throat, and the sound of her heightening passion seemed to arouse Steel even more. His manhood was heavy against her; heated, strong, wanting.

"My beard," he said, his voice raspy. "I'll scratch you."

"Shhh," she said, sinking her hands into his thick hair and bringing his mouth once again to hers.

Steel's tongue slipped into her mouth as his hand moved to the lacy waistband of her bikini panties. He slid his fingers under the elastic, stroking, caressing the velvety mound within his touch. It was heavenly torment, and Megan savored each sensation that swept through her.

"Megan," Steel said, taking a ragged breath, "let me see you. I need to see you, babe."

She raised her arms and allowed him to draw the jersey over her head and fling it onto the floor. His eyes raked over her breasts, the flat plane of her stomach, her femininity just barely concealed by the wispy material of her panties, to return to her face and the smoky hue of her green eyes.

"Lovely," he said. "So very beautiful. I want you, Megan. I want to make love to you."

"Yes," she whispered.

Steel shifted his body to rid himself of his underwear, and Megan instantly missed his weight, his heat. When he turned to her again, he rained a trail of nibbling kisses up her stomach to come at last to her breasts, his mouth seeking one, his hand the other. Megan arched her back to more fully receive the tantalizing sensations coursing within her. A liquid warmth started in the core of her femininity and swept through her, bringing a flush to her cheeks and Steel's name to her lips.

"Steel."

The sound of his own name being whispered with a voice thick with passion caused Steel's blood to pound through his veins and his manhood to surge against the lissome form beneath him. He moved upward to take possession of Megan's mouth in a kiss that was drugging in its intensity. Never had he desired a woman the way he did Megan. Never! There was nothing beyond this moment, beyond this woman so soft and warm and . . . his.

There were thoughts creeping from the inner chambers of his mind demanding to be heard, and he pushed them away, refused to listen. He would pay no credence to the questions, the doubts that lay just beneath the surface of his consciousness. Not now. Not yet. This was Megan. His Megan. He felt a protectiveness, a possessiveness, a need to give of himself in their union to assure her pleasure, rather than seek only his own gratification.

Steel felt his muscles tremble as Megan's fingertips trailed over his back. He strove for control, wishing to prolong the sweet agony of wanting, yet needing to bury himself deep within the honeyed warmth of her body. His mind held a fervent wish to make their coming together perfect for her, to give to her the essence of his being, his masculinity, power and strength. Never before had he registered such a driving desire to please, to see sated contentment on the face of the woman he held. These were new and startling emotions for Steel.

"Megan," he murmured. "Ah, Megan."

"Please, Steel, come to me. Please."

He moved over her in answer to her whispered plea, and the silver hawk around his neck swayed as if in flight across her breasts. She looked up into his ebony eyes and found what she was seeking in their depth: desire, warmth and tenderness. With a soft sigh of pleasure, she lifted to meet him as he entered her with a bold thrust of his manhood.

He slid his arm under her hips to bring her closer, to fill her, drive deep within her, and she was consumed by his heat and strength. And then it began. With movements matched as beautifully as the most carefully choreographed dance, they moved as one toward splendor.

"Steel!" Megan gasped.

"Yes! Hold on, Megan. I'm here, babe."

They held fast to each other, slowly returning from ecstasy... as one.

"Oh, Steel," Megan said, "I didn't know it could be so beautiful."

"Did I hurt you?" he asked, searching her face for an answer.

"No! It was so wonderful. *You* are wonderful. *We* are wonderful."

"That's a lot of wonderful," he said, smiling as he moved gently off her and pulled her close to his side. Perfect, he thought. For her, for him. Perfect. Megan was his.

"This silver hawk," Megan said, nestling it in her palm. "It must be special to you."

"Very. My grandfather gave it to me when I was a boy. I'll pass it on to... Well..."

"Your son?"

"Yeah," he said, kissing her on the forehead, "my son."

They lay quietly, each lost in their own thoughts. Finally, Steel sighed and ran his hand down his face.

"I have to get going," he said.

"You're still sick, Steel."

"Can't keep a good Indian down," he said, swinging his feet to the floor. "I've really got to hustle. I'll call you later."

"Steel?" Megan said inquiringly, scrambling to her knees as he began to pull on his clothes.

"I don't want to leave you," he said, "but I have to."

"You have to get to... your investment company?"

"Megan," he said, sitting on the edge of the bed to put on his socks and shoes. "I don't have time to explain now."

"Yes, all right," she said, sighing deeply.

Steel turned to look at Megan, saw the confusion on her face, the soft glow of her skin as she knelt before him, the wild disarray of her strawberry-blond hair. His heart quickened, and he felt the urge to draw her to him, tell her who he really was, talk to her for hours and make love to her for even more.

"I'll be back, Megan," he promised. "You believe me, don't you?"

"Yes, Steel, I believe you."

Steel brushed his lips across hers and then strode from the room. She saw the automatic gesture as he swept his hands over his back pockets, checking instinctively for what she knew was there. His wallet and the leather case that held his secret identity; the badge and card that said he was Lieutenant Steel Danner of the Los Angeles Police Department.

A chilling silence fell over the room, and Megan crept beneath the blankets on the bed, huddling in a ball like a frightened child.

Five

When Steel emerged into the crisp morning air, he pushed all thoughts of Megan from his mind and concentrated on Frankie Bodeen. Damn it, why had Frankie set his niece up in Megan's store? And why had Bodeen gone to Paris?

Steel went to his apartment, showered, shaved and dressed in clean jeans and a blue sweater. When he entered the office, he nodded at Casey, then sank wearily into his chair.

"You should have stayed home," Casey said.

"No. Any word on Bodeen?"

"I haven't had time to check this morning. Did you follow up on—well, forget it for now. You really look lousy."

"Megan lied," Steel said, his voice flat. "She wasn't born in L.A., never went to UCLA, nothing."

"I'm sorry."

"It doesn't mean she's connected to Bodeen."

"Ah, Steel, come on! It all fits! Bodeen is after fancy new stuff, Megan has an antique store, Clara Bodeen works there... What more do you want?"

"The truth," Steel said quietly, "and I'm going to get it."

"Good morning, gentlemen," Captain Meredith said, coming into the room. "Lord, Danner, you look like hell."

"Thanks," he muttered.

"He's sick," Casey said, "but try telling him he should be home in bed. Your scalp will be in jeopardy."

"Ahhn, the luxury of rank," the captain said. "Casey, take him home."

"Hey, now wait just a damn minute here!" Steel said, lunging to his feet. "Oh, man," he groaned, gripping the edge of the desk as a wave of dizziness swept over him.

"That's all," Casey said, getting up. "Let's go."

"No, I—"

"Stow it, Danner," the captain said. "Haul his butt out of here, Jones."

The expletives Steel cut loose with all the way to the car caused Casey to roll his eyes to the heavens. At Steel's apartment Casey announced he was hungry and headed for the kitchen as Steel slouched on the sofa and closed his eyes. A short time later, Casey hollered that it was time to eat.

"Eggs. Toast. Coffee. Sit," Casey said, when Steel entered the kitchen.

"Looks good," Steel said, sitting. "Damn, my body aches."

"Well, listen to this. It will take your mind off your deteriorating self. I called to see if the Fed in Paris had reported in. Bodeen didn't stay long over there. Messed around, then came on home."

"With what?" Steel asked, his fork halting in mid-air.

"Nothing."

"What?"

"*Nada*. Zilch. Zip," Casey said.

"Damn."

"He made no contacts, stayed in plain view and took pictures."

"Pictures?"

"Not of the Eiffel Tower, my son. Frankie Bodeen took pictures of antiques."

"Pictures of antiques," Steel said, squinting at the ceiling. "Why?"

"He told everybody who asked," Casey said. "His wife loves the junk, and with the pictures she can decide at her leisure what she wants."

"He doesn't have a wife!"

"*We* know that, and *he* knows that."

"It matches, Casey. Frank Sands told Megan he'd decide what she should get him as a gift for his wife. Bodeen is going to send Megan in to get him something he wants very badly."

"Customs goes over that stuff with a fine-tooth comb, Steel. Nothing gets into this country with false bottoms in drawers or whatever. There's been so many smuggling scams attempted with antiques in the past that customs and the Bureau have it down pat. Bodeen isn't that stupid."

"Pictures. Photographs of antiques. Why?" Steel said, smacking the table with his hand. "Oh, ow! Damn it!" he said, holding his head.

"That was bright. Well, I'm off. I'll have your car brought over. Give me your keys."

"In the movies the big, tough detective says, 'I'm going with you.' Guess what, Casey? I don't think I could move if my life depended on it."

After Casey had left, Steel pulled off his shoes and stretched out on the bed. Megan. Their lovemaking had been incredible, like nothing he'd experienced before. He hadn't wanted to leave her after what they'd shared. He's wanted to forget the world outside her door....

His meandering thoughts came to a halt as a sudden realization occurred to him. Brother, if anyone read his mind they'd accuse him of being in love with Megan! "Forget it!" he said aloud. "I'm not in love with Megan James!" Was he? He'd know if he were. Wouldn't he? Ah, hell, he was going to take a nap!

The day was a seemingly endless stretch of hours for Megan. Her heart raced each time the door to Memory Lane opened, and her spirits plummeted when Steel Danner did not enter. She skipped lunch to stay near the telephone and forced a lightness to her voice when the caller wasn't Steel.

Just after three o'clock, Megan wandered into her office and absently switched on the radio.

"The police officer who was hurt," the announcer said, "Lieutenant S.D. Tanner, was treated and released from the hospital, and is credited with saving the life of the child trapped in the burning building. The parents of the girl..."

"He said Lieutenant Tanner. Did he mean Danner?" Megan whispered, snapping off the radio. "Steel's hurt? Dear God, no!"

Megan snatched her purse from the desk drawer and ran to the outer room.

"Take over, Clara," Megan said. "I have to go out. Just lock up at closing if I'm not back."

"But—"

"Goodbye."

Ginger looked up to see a very lovely but very pale young woman standing in front of her desk.

"Yes? May I help you?" Ginger inquired.

"I must see Steel. I mean, Lieutenant Danner, please," Megan said.

"He isn't in, but his partner is. Could he be of assistance?"

"Partner?"

"Lieutenant Jones. Casey Jones."

"Yes," Megan said. "May I see Lieutenant Jones?"

"Sure. Through the squad room, down the hall, third door on your left."

"Thank you."

"Are you okay?" Ginger said, frowning.

"I hope so."

Megan was oblivious to the appreciative glances she received as she made her way across the squad room. At the designated door she knocked lightly, her hand trembling.

"Yeah!"

"Lieutenant Casey Jones?" Megan asked, stepping just inside the door.

"The same. And who are you?"

"Lieutenant, please tell me if he's been hurt. I have to know if he's all right."

"Whoa! Who? Who's hurt?"

"Steel. I'm Megan James."

"Hoo-boy," Casey said, jumping to his feet. "You know that Steel is a cop? How did you—"

"Casey! Is he dead?" Megan demanded, beginning to shake from head to toe.

"Hey, easy," Casey said, hurrying to Megan and sitting her gently on a chair. "Steel isn't dead. He's fine. Well, he's sort of sick, but nothing major. You're not going to faint on me here, are you?"

"No, I...I'm all right. I was just so frightened when I heard the news about the fire on the radio. I thought the policeman injured might have been Steel."

"Cops with the flu don't make the news," Casey said. "Man, you're really shook. If I didn't know better I'd think... Uh-oh. You are, aren't you?"

"Pardon me?"

"You're in love with Steel."

"No, of course, not."

"That's not what I'm reading in those green eyes of yours, but I won't argue the point. Come on."

"Where are we going?"

"To see Steel. It's truth time, Megan James. Everything up front."

Steel stirred on the bed at the first knock on the door and decided somewhere in his foggy state to ignore it. When the drumming continued, he swore repeatedly and pushed himself to his feet. His sweater had become too warm and he had pulled it off. With his jeans slung low on his hips, and his hand raking through his hair, he strode to the door and flung it open.

"Hi!" Casey said brightly. "Look who dropped in. Close your mouth and the door," he said, leading Megan by the elbow into the room.

"Megan?" Steel said quizzically.

"Oh, Steel," she said, her gaze riveted on his cloudy eyes and flushed skin.

"Megan? Casey?"

"Articulate group," Casey said. "I think we should all sit down."

"What in the hell is going on here!" Steel bellowed, coming out of his semi-trance.

"Good heavens," Megan said, covering her heart with her hand.

"Well, at least he's awake," Casey said. "Sit!"

"Casey, what have you done?" Steel asked, sitting.

"Nothing! Megan came to me. She knows you're a cop."

"You do?" Steel said, looking at Megan.

"Yes. When you were so sick I folded your clothes and your ID fell on the floor."

"Last night? Then you knew I was lying through my teeth and you let me ... Why?"

"Excuse me," Casey said, clearing his throat. "I do believe I will hasten forth to yon supermarket and get you orange juice, chicken soup and aspirin. Your cupboards are in sad shape. Cover the personal jazz while I'm gone, then we have the subject of this lady's credibility to discuss."

"My what?" Megan demanded as Casey left the apartment.

"Where were you born, Megan?" Steel asked quietly. "I want the truth this time."

"You checked up on me? Why, Steel?"

"Where were you born?"

"Oklahoma!" she said, tears filling her eyes. "On a farm where I watched my father die by inches. Oh, God, I hated that place! As soon as I could, I left, I ran. We struggled so much, and nothing ever came of it. There was no hope there, no dreams."

"Megan, honey—" he said, getting to his feet.

"No," she said, moving out of her chair and backing away from him. "I don't know what you want with me, but now you know about my past. The pennies. The pennies in the fountain. There was no magic fountain in Oklahoma."

"Oh, God," Steel moaned, closing the distance between them and pulling her into his arms. "Oh, Megan, forgive me."

"Please, Steel," she sobbed, "I've earned what I have. I haven't done anything wrong. I haven't!"

"I know, Megan. I'm here with you. No harm is going to come to you, I promise. Megan, look at me."

Megan raised her head, tears streaming down her face and gazed into Steel's eyes.

"Megan," he said, cradling her face in his hands and brushing her tears away with his thumbs, "Megan, you've become very important to me. Very important. Nothing, *nothing*, is ever going to hurt you again."

"Oh, Steel."

He claimed her mouth in a kiss that was long and powerful, and she trembled in his arms. A knock at the door brought a frown to Steel's face as he raised his head, then strode across the room to pull the door open none too gently.

"Hi," Casey said. "How's life?"

"Take a hike, Jones," Steel growled.

"Sorry, buddy," Casey said, entering the apartment with a grocery bag in his arms. "We have a prob, remember?"

"Yeah," Steel said, "Frankie Bodeen."

Six

Before we go any further, Steel," Megan said, "I've got to know how you're feeling."

"I'm fine," he said, pulling her down next to him on the sofa. "Good as new."

"I figure he's a breath away from having pneumonia," Casey said. "But, yeah, other than that he's fine."

"Oh, thanks, Jones," Steel said, rolling his eyes to the heavens.

"Just trying to be helpful," Casey said, shrugging.

"Oh, dear heaven," Megan said, "I think Casey's right. You do have pneumonia. You've got to see a doctor."

"Later, maybe," Steel said. "Look, we really have to cover some things here. Have you ever heard the name Frankie Bodeen?"

"No, only Clara Bodeen, who works for me."

"Frank Sands is Frankie Bodeen," Steel said. "Clara is his niece."

"Frank Sands? The man in the restaurant?" Megan said, puzzled. "But why would he use a different name? I thought all he wanted was a gift for his wife. I guess I'm being very naive, right? Something terrible is going on, and you thought I was involved because I had lunch with him. Who is Frankie Bodeen?"

"Well?" Steel said, grinning at Casey.

"Hell, man, I tried to tell you she was squeaky clean in this, but would you listen? Nope. There you were, hell-bent on... Welcome aboard, Megan James. And to answer your question, Frankie is a big-time drug dealer we've whittled down to size for a while. So, he's after fresh meat. Short and sweet, honey, it looks like he's going to move something big, using your store as a cover."

"What?" Megan shrieked. "A crook jeopardizing the reputation of Memory Lane? The very idea! The nerve of that man! Well, he can just forget it. I won't allow it."

"Oh, okay," Casey chuckled, "we'll tell him."

"You're so cute," Steel said, smiling, then kissed her on the tip of her nose.

"How did you meet Clara Bodeen?" Casey asked. "Did you advertise for a salesclerk?"

"No," Megan said, "I wasn't sure I wanted to take on the expense of another salary. But as it became apparent that my clients were speaking more and more of sending me on buying trips, I began to consider the possibility of hiring an assistant."

"And up pops Clara," Steel said.

"Yes. She walked into Memory Lane bubbling with excitement and very knowledgeable about antiques. I decided it was fate and I hired her."

"Nicely done," Steel said, nodding. "Bodeen is slick. Let me guess. Clara wanted to know everything about running an antique store because she hoped to have her own someday."

"Yes, she said it had been a lifelong dream."

"And you taught her how the books are set up, where you get your info on upcoming auctions, what you've bought from where, the whole nine yards."

"Yes, and she learned very quickly."

"So, Clara ends up knowing exactly how Memory Lane operates, including your personal habits, the hours you work, how you document everything. Right?"

"Yes, Steel, she's very bright and so eager. It's hard to believe she was using me like this."

"Megan," Casey said, "have you ever heard of anyone taking pictures of antiques before they come up for auction?"

"Well, no, but it's not that unreasonable. There are brochures that go out before a sale with photographs, but they don't show true quality very well. I suppose if someone had a very expensive camera they could capture the fine detail of the piece and take their time deciding what they wanted to go after."

"Interesting," Steel said, pushing himself to his feet, waiting for the dizziness to pass, then beginning to pace the floor.

"Beddy-bye time, Steel," Casey said. "You're turning into a gray Indian again."

"In a minute," he said. "Who can we get to replace Megan at Memory Lane?"

"What!" Megan and Casey exclaimed in unison.

"I want her out of there, Casey," Steel grated, his jaw tight.

"Are you nuts?" Casey demanded, lunging to his feet. "She has to be there so Frank Sands can contact her."

"No!"

"Steel, we pull Megan, and Bodeen will smell a rat. She stays!"

"She goes!"

"Listen, you stubborn Indian, I'm telling you that Megan—"

"Shut up!" Megan yelled, shocking both men into stunned silence. "I *am* in this room, remember? Did it ever occur to you two that I might have a say in this? Memory Lane is mine. I've worked so hard to turn it into something special. No one, *no one*, has the right to attempt to destroy it. I won't be driven away by a man like Bodeen. I'm never running again, not from him, or anyone. I'm staying in my store and in my world. It's where I belong. As the Indians say, 'I have spoken.'"

Steel and Casey looked at Megan, then at each other, then at Megan again. She folded her arms over her breasts and stared up at them, a determined tilt to her chin.

"I think," Casey said, a smile tugging at his lips, "that you have your hands full here, buddy. Look, let's give it a rest for now. You need to go back to bed, Steel. I mean it, you're out on your feet and you'd better get shipshape before this thing goes down. Megan, are you staying here?"

"Of course, she's staying here," Steel said. "I mean, aren't you, Megan?"

"My car is at the police station."

"Give me your keys," Casey said. "I'll have it brought over. The uniforms are going to start charging me shuttle service. I'll check in with you later, Steel. Megan, I'm glad you're on the scene, honey. Why you'd want to hang out with Blade of Steel Danner I'll never know, but different strokes for different folks. He's got a rotten temper, he's a real slob around the house, and—"

"Goodbye, Jones," Steel said.

"Right," Casey said, accepting Megan's keys. "See ya. Bed, Steel. Now!"

"In his next life, he should be a mother," Steel muttered as Casey left the apartment.

A silence fell; a lovely stillness that seemed to cast a rosy glow over the room. Steel reached out his hand and Megan placed hers in it, rising to her feet to move into his arms. She nestled close to his warm, bare chest as Steel held her tightly, one arm around her shoulders, his hand on her hair as he pressed her head to his shoulder. They simply stood there, drinking in the feel and aroma of each other.

"You're so special," Steel finally said quietly. "I'm glad I found you, Megan."

"I'm glad, too. More than you know. You've got to rest now."

"I suppose," he said, not moving.

"Go to bed."

"Come with me."

"No."

"Just be close, near, okay? I want to make love to you so badly, but I'm temporarily out of commission. Very temporarily. We'll lie there. Together."

"Yes, all right."

In the bedroom Steel stretched out on the bed and closed his eyes with a weary sigh. Megan took off her dress and draped it on a chair, revealing a pale-blue full-length slip. She crawled next to Steel and rested her head on his shoulder. As his hand encountered the silky fabric of her slip, his eyes shot open.

"What is that?" he asked.

"My slip. I didn't want to wrinkle my dress."

"Ah, man, you don't play fair. How am I going to rest when you're lying there like that?"

"Close your eyes and you won't see me."

"Ha!"

"Go to sleep."

"Kiss me first."

"No."

"Yes," he said, shifting his weight to claim her mouth in a fiery kiss.

Megan's desires spiraled instantly as Steel's tongue delved deep into her mouth. He cared for her! she thought. Blade of Steel Danner really did care for *her*, and the truth brought tears of joy prickling at the back of her eyes.

"Megan, I want you," Steel said, his voice raspy. "I need you, babe. I need to make love to you now, this minute."

"But you're sick."

"I'm not dead," he growled, his lips finding hers again.

Steel Danner was very much alive, Megan thought dreamily.

Their lovemaking was slow, and sweet, and beautiful. Steel kissed and caressed her in a languorous journey that brought a purring moan from her throat. Her hands trailed over his sculpted muscles to stroke and touch his taut, bronzed skin. His manhood was a bold announcement of his need of her, and she felt cherished, special, rare.

"Megan," Steel said, lifting his head from the fullness of her breasts, "I want you."

"Yes, Steel. Now."

Their union brought an unspoken bond of trust. The doubts and fears, the shadows of deception and unanswered questions, were swept away and replaced by rainbow colors and a liquid warmth that coursed through them, carrying them to their place of ecstasy.

Steel kissed Megan deeply, then moved away and tucked her close to his side.

From that day forward, Megan thought, her pennies in the fountain would be for them, for their happiness. She loved Steel Danner. The last whisper of doubt regarding her feelings for this man were whisked away. She was in love with him. "Go to sleep, Steel," she said gently.

"Yeah, okay, just for a little while. I . . . really . . . am beat."

In the next moment Steel's breathing was steady and even, and Megan smiled as she realized he was already asleep. Her gaze traveled over his rugged length from head to toe, savoring the sight of his masculine physique. She suddenly recalled the icy fear she'd felt when she'd believed it was Steel's name she'd heard on the radio.

Steel was a detective, a police officer, she thought. His life's work was dangerous. But being a cop was the choice Steel had made, and she would accept it. He had passed no censure on her childhood of endless struggles and poverty. They were coming to each other as they were, in honesty and trust, and it would be the foundation on which they would build their existence. She loved him. It sounded so simple. He did not love her, but his feelings for her were growing, and for now it was enough.

After dressing, Megan explored the kitchen and found Casey had been right—the selection was slim. The freezer full of TV dinners held no appeal, and she decided that bacon and eggs would be the extent of the dinner menu when Steel awoke.

She wandered back into the living room and studied the books on Steel's rather jumbled bookcase. She would, she decided, read a detective novel. Since she was involved in this fiasco with Frankie Bodeen she might as well get some pointers on how the good guys caught the bad buys. And *she* was one of the good guys.

To her disappointment, there were no detective stories in Steel's collection. His library consisted of biographical works on American Indians and a large selection of well-worn science fiction paperbacks. Megan settled for a thick volume on the life of Cochise, the famous Apache Indian chief, and she curled up in the corner of the sofa to read.

Over an hour later, she was so deeply engrossed in the book that the feathery kiss planted on her cheek caused her to jump in surprise.

"Steel!" she said. "Goodness, you startled me. How are you feeling?"

"Much better," he said, sitting down next to her. "What do you have there? Cochise? Now he was one tough Indian."

"It says here that he met with General Gordon Granger at Canada Alamosa in 1866 to talk peace. Cochise said, 'I have drunk of these waters and they have cooled me. I—'"

" 'I do not want to leave here,' " Steel said, completing the quote.

"You've memorized this?"

"I've always liked those words. This may sound corny, Megan, but I feel that way about you. I've found you, and I do not want to leave here, leave the world I have with you. You've become very important to me very quickly."

"I'm so glad, Steel," she said softly, placing her hand on his rugged cheek.

Steel turned his head to kiss her palm, then took her hand between his two large ones and placed it on his thigh, the heat radiating up Megan's arm and across her breasts.

"I think you're a helluva woman for having accomplished what you have," he said.

"Then you should be able to understand why Memory Lane means what it does to me, and why Frankie Bodeen won't drive me away. I'm not leaving my store."

"It would only be until this is over."

"No, I won't go! Besides, you heard Casey. Bodeen will suspect something if I suddenly disappear."

"Casey isn't always right."

"But he is this time, and you know it."

"Yeah, I suppose," Steel said, frowning. "Bodeen is no dummy. But, damn it, I don't want you caught up in this! It could get dangerous, Megan!"

"So protect me," she said, shrugging. "That's what policemen are for, isn't it?"

"Yours is feeling rocky as hell," he said. "I didn't even protect *myself* from germs! Good thing my sister Roddy doesn't know about this. She'd be here fussing all over me."

"Roddy? Is that short for something, too?"

"Waving Goldenrod. You're dealing with very authentic Indians here, my sweet," he said smiling at her.

In the next instant Steel kissed her, and she melted against him, savoring his taste and aroma, his strength, his very being. Their desires soared instantly as the kiss intensified, then Steel slowly, reluctantly, released her.

"Food," he said, close to her lips. "Big juicy steaks."

"Bacon and eggs. Your pantry is a disaster."

"Ugh. Casey already stuffed one meal like that into me today. Okay, I'll survive. I'll put on a shirt and whip up the toast."

"Deal. You and Casey are very close, aren't you?"

"In our line of work you have to be. Are you having a problem with me being a detective?"

"No. I've accepted it because it's a part of who you are. I'm not saying it doesn't worry me because of the dangers, but I won't cry and moan about it. Everyone has a right to choose their own path and you've done that. I understand what that means."

"Thank you, babe. I'll get a shirt," he said, heading for the bedroom.

Steel pulled on a dark-blue cotton shirt and started to button it, but he stopped halfway up his chest. He blinked slowly, then drew a steadying breath. He was in love with Megan! he thought. Blade of Steel Danner, who moved through life alone, one step back and away from emotional involvements except for his grandfather, Roddy, Brian and Casey, was in love. It had hit him like a ton of bricks, and he suddenly felt like a kid on his birthday. He loved his Megan!

Megan. Man, what a lousy childhood she'd had. But she'd emerged from her life of unhappiness to become a beautiful woman of grace and elegance, a sharp business person who was respected in the world of the affluent. And Megan was his. Wasn't she? Would she come to love him in return? Was she interested in love and marriage? Would she want to have his son, the one he'd give the silver hawk to? Ah, hell, he'd worry about that stuff later. For now he'd get used to the idea of being in love. So far, it was terrific!

"Eggs are almost ready," Megan said, when Steel entered the kitchen. "Here, sit and eat this," she said, setting plates on the table and sitting down opposite him. "I'll clean up the kitchen and then go on home."

"Home? Why?"

"Because you still need a lot of rest and I have to work tomorrow."

"You could spend the night here, then get up early enough to go to your place and change before Memory Lane opens."

"Nope. Look what happened when I rested with you earlier. If I get out of here you'll have to sleep, like it or not."

"You're cold," he said frowning. "Heartless. I'm a sick, sick man. I need care, and attention, and—"

"Eat your eggs."

"Right. Megan, when you go to the store tomorrow, you've got to act very naturally around Clara. She mustn't sense any change in you or... Damn, I hate this. I don't want you there!"

"Steel, don't," Megan said quietly. "Memory Lane is mine and I've got to protect it."

"And *you* are mine! I've got to protect you. I'm going to sit Casey down and come up with a plan to—"

"No! I'm not leaving my store! You can't force me to, and I don't want to argue with you about it. It's the only way to catch Bodeen and you know it. The details of the cops and robbers junk are up to you and Casey. As for me, I'm running an antique business and one of my customers happens to be Frank Sands."

"Cops and robbers?" Steel said, grinning. "That's pretty high-tech jargon."

"Whatever," she shrugged. "The fact remains that I'm staying."

"Oh, good. Then I can add an ulcer to my list of infirmities."

"That's okay. You like milk anyway."

"You're not a kind person, Megan."

"But you like me."

"Yes, I like you," he said, reaching for her hand, "but it goes deeper than that. I love you, Megan."

Tears misted Megan's eyes as she smiled at him. "And I love you, Steel," she said, her voice hushed. "I love you very, very much."

"I'll be damned," he said, getting to his feet and walking around the table. "You do?"

"I do," she said, moving into his embrace. "Oh, yes, I do."

The kiss they shared was long and powerful and desires soared. Steel groaned when Megan finally wiggled out of his arms and firmly stated that they had a kitchen to clean. But somewhere between cleaning the kitchen and leaving Steel's apartment, Megan got sidetracked. She was pulled into Steel's arms and kissed with such passionate intensity that her knees trembled and her heart raced. When he circled her shoulders with his arm and led her to the bedroom, she voiced no objection; she simply smiled up at him with a dreamy expression on her face. Their coming together was splendor and ecstasy, giving and taking. And over and over, they declared their love.

Steel insisted on tugging on his clothes and seeing Megan safely to her car. He reached his long arm under the seat to find the key where he knew the uniformed officer would have left it, handing it to Megan with a deep bow and a smug smile. Then he drew her into his arms and kissed her deeply before helping her into the car. As Megan drove away, Steel watched until she had disappeared from view, then walked slowly back into the building. Inside the living room he sat on the sofa and picked up the receiver to the telephone, dialing the familiar number.

"Jones," Casey answered on the second ring.

"It's Steel. I know this is your time to be with your kids so I'll make it quick."

"The boys are in the bathtub pretending they're submarines. Sally's watching them so you have my undivided attention. How are you feeling?"

"Fine."

"Your Megan is A-OK, Steel. I'm happy for you."

"Thanks, Casey. She's . . . well, really something. I love her a lot, Casey."

"I'd already figured that out, Steel. So, okay, lay it on me. You want Megan out of the store."

"She won't budge."

"Good for her. Steel, I know you love her, but surely you see we can't pull her out now. Bodeen will slip right through our fingers."

"How are we going to protect her, Casey? I can't camp out there all day without looking fishy. Remember, Clara is reporting back to Bodeen, and she's already very wary of me. It won't wash if I stick like glue."

"We can't make plans at this point. We won't even know what the setup is until Frank Sands contacts

Megan. Drop by Memory Lane once in a while so Clara gets used to seeing you, but don't overdo it. For now, we wait for Sands, and Megan goes about her business as if everything is hunky-dory.''

"The good old hurry-up-and-wait.''

"Yep. Hey, you need this time to get back in shape. You're on R and R, so says our beloved captain. He doesn't want to see your ugly mug at the station for a few days.''

"Wonderful,'' Steel muttered.

"See ya, Steel. Your Megan is a helluva nice lady.''

"I know. Night, Casey.''

Steel replaced the receiver and scowled deeply. Then for lack of anything better to do, he went to bed.

The next morning, Megan wanted to call Steel to see how he was feeling, but was afraid she would wake him. She left her apartment and drove to the usual parking lot across the street from the park opposite Memory Lane. At the fountain a gentle smile formed on her lips, and she held the penny tightly in her hand before dropping it into the water. She made a wish centered on Steel, their love, their tomorrows. As she gazed into the sprinkling rainbow-colored spray, Steel's face flashed before her eyes and she wanted to run back to her car and hurry to his apartment where she could be the recipient of his kiss and touch.

With a whimsical sigh, she turned and headed toward Memory Lane. As she entered the store she glanced around, seeing the familiar objects just as she'd left them. But *she* was changed. She had dashed out the door in icy fear after hearing what she had thought was Steel's name on the radio and now returned as a woman in love who was loved in kind.

But, she decided firmly, she couldn't go around with a silly grin on her face or Clara would sense, see, that something was going on in Megan's life that hadn't been there before. It would be business as usual and Clara would be none the wiser.

"Frank Sands," Megan whispered. "When will he call? What will happen next?"

Seven

___

"Damn it, Steel," Casey yelled. "What are you doing here?"

"I was going crazy in that apartment. What's the word?" Steel asked sinking into his chair behind his desk.

"Nothing. Quiet as a mouse. It's lunchtime. Let's go eat before Meredith spots you and raises hell."

"Yeah, okay. I haven't talked to Megan for a while. I was at Memory Lane yesterday. I don't think it's a good idea to go back again today."

"You're pouting. I'll buy you a hamburger. That'll cheer you up."

At a small café Steel ordered three hamburgers, French fries, coffee and milk.

"Hungry?" the waitress asked, smiling at him coyly.

"There's a lot of me to fill up."

"You can say that again, honey," she said, wiggling away.

"You'll have to knock that off now, you know," Casey said, having settled for two hamburgers and coffee.

"Eating?"

"Flirting."

"I wasn't flirting, Casey!"

"You were born flirting! But, my boy, those days are over. A man in love has eyes only for his beloved."

"Do tell," Steel said, frowning. "Looking is not touching, Jones. I'd never cheat on Megan. Hell, I love her."

"Which blows my mind. Steel Danner in love. Are you planning on marrying her?"

"I'm thinking about it. I don't know, Casey, she's pretty independent. She's been alone a long time, has her own business. Maybe she's not interested in marriage and babies right now."

"So, ask and find out."

"Hey, I'm just getting used to the idea that I'm in love! Marriage is a very big step. You're talking mortgage, station wagon, diapers and junk. I want a son, I really do. A daughter would be all right, too, but the whole picture is a little overwhelming. I think I'll just take this slow and easy for a while."

"Does Megan have any hang-ups about you being a cop?"

"No, not at all," Steel said. "She accepts me and my work, no questions asked."

"Ah, hell, you've got it made. Marry her, you fool, before she gets away. You can't pass on that silver hawk to a son who isn't born. Speaking of which, Sally says we should have another baby before the boys get much older. She wants them to all grow up together.''

"I suppose you'll go for twins again,'' Steel chuckled.

"I'm a very virile man. So? Are you going to marry Megan?''

"I don't know. I need some time to adjust to having a woman in my life full time. I've been single a lot of years, Casey.''

"That's true, so marry her and get on with your lives together.''

"Heads up, boys,'' the waitress said. "Plates are hot. Will there be anything else?'' she added, looking directly at Steel.

"Got a phone in here?'' Steel asked. "I need to call my wife.''

"No!'' the girl said, and flounced away.

"I'm proud of you, Danner,'' Casey said, whopping him on the shoulder. "You're getting the hang of this already.''

Steel laughed, and the two men ate in silence for several minutes.

"Steel,'' Casey finally said, "have you settled down about Megan staying at the store and seeing this thing through with Bodeen?''

"Not really. I get a knot in my gut every time I think of her being involved. She's adamant about staying, though, and somewhere in my mind I guess I realize it's the only thing to do. If it weren't for Clara being there I could hang around Memory Lane more. If Clara gets suspicious at all and tells Bodeen, he's liable to run a check on me and blow the whole thing.''

"Look, whatever Bodeen wants he's going to send Megan to get it at an auction or something. We can have plainclothes guys coming out of the woodwork when that happens. Same goes for when she makes delivery. Then we nab him.''

"But what does he want? And if he saw it in Paris, how in the hell is he going to smuggle it through customs? And if he does manage to get it in, why not just run with it instead of using Megan? Have you noticed there's a lot of loose ends here?''

"You're not kidding. If it wasn't Bodeen, I'd say it was a sloppy deal, but with him in charge you know it's fine-tuned. Trick is for us to figure it all out.''

"Without Megan getting hurt," Steel growled. "I swear, Casey, if—''

"She'll be fine. Nothing is going to happen to Megan James, Blade of Steel. I have spoken. Go home and take a nap.''

"I'm sick to death of naps!''

Much to his own annoyance, Steel realized he was tired when he returned to the station, so with a muttered goodbye to Casey, he headed back to his apartment. In the living room he stared at the telephone for a long moment, and then with a growly expletive, picked up the receiver and dialed.

"Good afternoon. Memory Lane.''

"Megan? Steel. Clara hanging around?''

"Yes.''

"Then play it loose, like I'm a customer. I assume there's been no word from Frank Sands?''

"No.''

"Okay. Want to go out to dinner tonight?''

"I'm sorry, sir, but that particular item was recently damaged and is being restored.''

"I'm not damaged!''

"I saw it myself. It's such a shame, but I feel confident it will be good as new. Would you settle for something else in the interim?"

"Damn it, Megan, quit being cute! We're going out to dinner!"

"That's impossible, sir. Perhaps I could drop a brochure off to you."

"Come here? There's nothing to eat."

"I'd be happy to bring it along."

"Oh. Well . . . steaks?"

"If you prefer."

"What I prefer, Megan James, is your soft, warm body next to mine in my bed. Is that on the menu?"

"That's part of our service, sir," Megan said, feeling heat creep onto her cheeks.

"Sold. I'll see you later. I love you, Megan."

"Then I'd say we're in complete agreement. Goodbye . . . sir."

"Bye, sexy," Steel said, smiling as he hung up. Yep, she was one helluva woman and he loved her, he thought smugly. Marriage. There was something to be said about coming home to welcoming arms instead of an empty apartment. He could learn to pick up his socks. But what about privacy? There were times when he needed to be alone, blank his mind, just tune out of the crummy side of life he dealt with every day. What happened to a man's space when he was married? Did he have to explain everything he did and why he did it? Would he be accountable to Megan for the hours he wasn't with her? "Hell," Steel said, and headed for the bedroom to take a nap.

Megan had replaced the receiver and then cleared her throat as desire tingled throughout her. Even the sound of Steel's voice had a disconcerting effect on her. Oh, how she loved him, she thought. She was half of a whole now, not truly complete until she was with Steel. Memory Lane was hers and she treasured it, but it took a second seat behind her love for Steel Danner. The store was running smoothly, making a profit, and with the hiring of a competent assistant once Clara could be gotten rid of, Megan could oversee the operation of the store and still devote herself to Steel and a baby and...a baby? Their child? Hers and Steel's? Oh, yes, that's what she wanted, to be Steel's wife, the mother of the son he'd give the silver hawk to with loving pride.

But how did Steel feel about marriage? About a commitment for a lifetime? He loved her, wanted her with him, was fiercely protective, but marriage? Maybe tomorrow she'd drop two pennies in the fountain and nudge her dreams on their way.

"Mrs. Pendleman is here," Clara said. "She wants to see the Mary Gregory vases you got in, but insists on dealing with you."

"I'll be right there, Clara."

"Nobody trusts me," Clara said.

"I can't imagine why," Megan said sarcastically under her breath as she headed to the front of the store.

When Megan had not arrived at the apartment by six-thirty, Steel began to pace the floor. At six-forty-five he was swearing in a steady stream, and at five minutes before seven he was worried sick. When Megan knocked at the door at seven o'clock, he flung it open.

"Where in the hell have you been?" he roared.

"May I come in?" Megan said, frowning.

"What? Oh, yeah, sure. Give me that bag. I was really worried about you," he said, shutting the door.

"So you yell at me? Nice guy. I had to go to the grocery store, remember? Then I got caught up in the rush hour traffic."

"Oh."

"You're in a terrific mood," Megan said, walking into the kitchen.

Steel set the bag on the counter, then reached out and grasped Megan's shoulders, turning her toward him.

"I'm sorry," he said. "I'm just not used to being cooped up, and it was getting so late that I started to worry."

"You're forgiven," she said, smiling. "A kiss would be nice."

"It's the least I can do," he said, lowering his mouth to hers.

The kiss was long and passionate, and Megan was trembling when Steel finally released her.

"How are you feeling?" she asked breathlessly.

"Not too bad. I think I'll kiss you again."

"No way. At this rate we won't have dinner till midnight."

"Or not at all," he said, reaching for her.

"Nope," she said, wiggling away from him. "It's food time. It will help you get your strength back."

"Will I need it?" he asked, grinning at her as he leaned against the counter.

"You certainly will, Blade of Steel. I missed you terribly today."

"How's wonderful Clara?" he said as Megan began to prepare the meal.

"Okay. I just acted normally and went about my business. I will admit my heart races every time the phone rings because I think it might be Frank Sands."

"He's never come into Memory Lane?"

"No, he called and asked me to meet him for lunch."

"He's really being cautious, wants absolutely no tie-in with the store. I sure wish I knew what he's after. Are there any special auctions coming up? You know, the biggy of the year or something?"

"No, just the usual."

"Damn, no clues at all. The next move is Bodeen's, and all we can do is wait. Hold it. That day we had lunch you said you sometimes go to foreign countries to buy things. Have you been anywhere recently?"

"I was in Paris two months ago."

"What?" Steel questioned, straightening.

"One of my clients paid my expenses to go to a special exhibition over there. It was the memorabilia from the movies made by Henri DuPont, the famous French movie star who recently died. The only value is sentimental, but there's a big market for that type of item."

"Did you buy anything?"

"Yes, but it was a rather unusual situation. The trustees of the estate agreed to leave the display open to the public for a while. Some of the pieces will be sold in Paris, the rest have been purchased and will come to the States. The piece I bought will clear through an auctioning house here later."

"What kind of piece?"

"Mrs. Morrison is absolutely thrilled. It's the mirror from the naughty flick, *Le miroir magie*. She has an obsession about Henri DuPont. She's slightly eccentric, but I adore her."

"Tell me about the mirror," Steel said.

"It's gawdy, in my opinion. It's eight by ten inches, and has a frame encrusted with tacky-looking colored jewels. Paste, of course. Henri's lover used to hold in-depth conversations with herself gazing into the thing."

"Interesting," Steel said, staring at the ceiling. "Very interesting."

"Whatever," Megan said, shrugging her shoulders.

After dinner Steel helped load the dishwasher, then pulled Megan down next to him on the sofa and kissed her deeply. As he lifted his head, he smiled at her gently and wove his fingers through her hair.

"I love your eyes when they're warm like they are now," Megan said. "At times they're so cold, distant, almost frightening."

"Don't ever be afraid of me, Megan. I'm going to take care of you, protect you, and I'll never hurt you."

"I didn't mean physically. There are other kinds of hurt and pain."

"I know that. I would never intentionally do anything to make you cry. I've never been in love before, Megan, and I have a feeling I don't understand all the facets of it. I'm used to being alone and not answering to anyone. I don't like the idea of having to be accountable for my time, but yet when you were late getting here I nearly went crazy. I felt as though I had the right to know exactly where you were. Talk about double standards. I'm really blowing it here."

"I think those things just naturally fall into place when two people love each other, Steel. A foundation of trust is built and it grows from there. I haven't been in love before either, but I'm sure that's how it works. You and I are still very new."

"I don't feel we are. It's as though I've known you for a lifetime. I just can't get a handle on my role. I'm not sure I know how to be in love."

"Wing it," she advised merrily.

"Would you get serious?"

"No. I love you, Steel, and I adore being in love. It makes me feel warm inside. Can't we just love each other and grow together?"

"I like to do things right," he said, frowning.

"There's no rule book for this, no training school. Give us a chance. We've only begun to understand each other. We'll—"

"Hell, the phone," Steel said, reaching behind him for the receiver. "Danner."

"Casey. Rick Tulley was working undercover on that special assignment and..."

"Yeah?"

"Steel, we just got word that his cover was blown, and he's dead."

"I'm on my way," Steel said, slamming the receiver into place and getting to his feet in the same motion.

"Steel?" Megan questioned as he pulled on his shoulder holster and checked the clip in his gun.

"What?" he asked, his jaw tight and his eyes cold and angry.

"You have to go out?"

"Yeah. Can you get home okay?"

"Yes, or I can wait here for you."

"I'll probably be gone all night. You'd better go home."

"All right. Was that Casey on the phone?"

"Yeah. Something's come up. I don't have time to get into it, Megan," he said, kissing her quickly before yanking on his jacket. "I'll call you when I can. See ya."

"Good night," she said softly as the door closed behind him. "Take good care of yourself, Detective Danner. Please."

Steel's jaw was aching before he had driven a mile, and he only then realized how tightly he had clenched it.

Rick was dead. That's how fast it could happen, Steel thought, shaking his head. A cop kissed his lady good-bye, left the house and had no way of knowing if he'd be back! "Damn it!" he ground out.

The police station was crowded with both plain-clothes and uniformed officers. Steel made his way through the throng to stand in front of Casey.

"Well?" Steel asked, his tone sharp.

"Nothing," Casey said. "No clues. Nobody's squealing."

Steel drew a steadying breath and looked at the ceiling for a long moment, striving to control his anger, his raging hate. Rick was dead, and there was no trace of him left behind. No wife. No children. Nothing. There was no son to carry on his name. What had been the purpose of his life? But what if he'd been married? His wife would be shattered, so damn alone. Megan. God, what if that happened to Megan? What if he were gunned down, leaving Megan, maybe even with a child to raise? Day after day, night after night, she'd be alone!

"Steel?" Casey questioned.

"Yeah," he said quietly, "I hear you, Casey."

"So, we're up to bat. Ready to play the game?"

"I suppose," Steel said wearily. "Lord, this is sick."

"Yeah, well, the jungle stinks," Casey said.

"See ya," Steel muttered, then strode out of the building to his car. How long would Megan cry if he were killed? he wondered. What pain would she suffer when she reached for him in the night and he wasn't there? How would she tell his son?

Steel slid behind the wheel of the car and crossed his arms over the steering wheel, resting his forehead on his hands, which were clenched into tight fists. Anger flowed through his veins like hot, searing lava; fury and frustration and raw hate like none he had ever felt before. His reaction to Rick's death jarred him, shook him to the inner core. He'd seen his friends die before. He had mourned their deaths and joined his peers to bring the killers to justice.

But now, with Rick, Steel saw more. Where Rick had been was a void, an empty place, for no woman had been his wife nor bore his child. But what if Rick had been a family man? And what if Steel became a family man?

Steel envisioned Megan. He saw her alone and weeping, clutching their child to her breast. She'd call to Steel to come to her, erase the ache and tell her it had been a mistake, that he was alive and would never leave her, that he would fulfill his promise to protect and care for her for all their days.

But Steel could not do that if he were dead.

A cacophony of voices screamed in Steel's mind as he started the car and drove to the district of the city where he would find the ones he was seeking. His gun felt like an unbearable weight beneath his jacket. He knew that a similar weapon would be held by an evil force, who would pull the trigger with no hesitation. And when that happened, Megan would cry. Steel had no right to make Megan cry. He felt torn in two, ripped apart. A section of him felt relief that Rick had been single, unencumbered, but yet, what had been the point of Rick's life?

Steel went through the night in a semi-trance, feeling like a robot that had been programmed to perform a duty. The cold, menacing look in Steel's dark eyes, the low, flat tone to his voice, the crackling tension emanating from his massive body, spoke a message of danger, of power, of strength, waiting for an invitation to be unleashed.

At eight in the morning, Steel signed his name to the last of the reports and shoved the papers at the desk sergeant. Steel was numb with fatigue. He wanted to go home, wash the stink of the city from his body and sleep. Just . . . sleep.

"Steel," Casey said, coming up beside him. "Rough night, huh?"

"Yeah."

"Want to get some breakfast?"

"No, Casey. Go home to your wife and kids. That's where you belong. That's where Rick belongs . . . home."

"I've never seen you like this, Steel. We've lost men before and it's lousy, but—"

"Go home, Casey."

"Yeah, okay. I'll talk to you later."

"Yeah. See ya," Steel said as he left the office and headed for home.

After returning to his apartment, Steel took a shower, then collapsed naked on the bed, falling instantly into a deep, dreamless sleep. When he woke in the middle of the afternoon, he was instantly alert, his mind centered on one name, one image.

Megan. Her voice, wavy hair, laughter, her face, flashed before his eyes. He saw her happy expression crumble with grief should something happen to him. Her world shattering into a million pieces. A handful of pennies, dozens of pennies a day in her wishing fountain, could not prevent it from happening when his number came up. Each time he walked out the door he couldn't promise he'd be back. He'd lived with that knowledge for years, accepted it long ago.

But never before had he loved.

Eight

Steel sat in the park until he saw Clara leave Memory Lane, then he headed across the street just as Megan was dropping the last bamboo curtain into place on the windows.

"Steel," she said, smiling brightly, "what a nice surprise. I've been thinking about you all day."

"Hello, Megan," he said quietly. "I hope you didn't have any problems getting home last night."

"No, of course not. Steel," she said, walking to where he stood, "is something wrong?"

"Megan, I—" he started, and then stopped speaking as he reached out and pulled her roughly into his arms, holding her tightly as he buried his face in the fragrant cloud of her hair.

Megan pressed her hands against his back as her breasts were crushed by the rock-hard wall of his chest. She could feel the tension emanating from him; rigid, coiled, gripping him like a vise. Questions screamed in her mind, but she kept silent. Moments passed and still he held her. Then she felt his muscles beneath her hands relax slightly as he drew a shuddering breath. Megan tilted her head back to look anxiously into his eyes, searching for a clue to his obvious distress.

"Steel?" she asked.

His answer was a long, searing kiss, almost punishing in its intensity as his mouth moved urgently over hers. And then the kiss gentled into a soft, sensuous embrace that brought a quiet moan from Megan's throat.

"I'm sorry," Steel said, lifting his head. "Did I hurt you?"

"No, no, you didn't hurt me, but what—"

"Let's get out of here. We'll go to dinner, okay? Someplace quiet, just the two of us."

"Yes, fine. I'll get my purse," she said, hurrying to her office. Oh, dear heaven, what was wrong with him? she thought. There was an emotion in his eyes she couldn't read, a slight franticness to his voice. She wouldn't push him. She'd be patient and allow him to explain his almost frightening mood when he was ready. If he chose to do so at all.

Steel selected a cozy restaurant that was rustic rather than fancy to accommodate his attire of jeans and sweater. They were shown to a quiet table in the corner where they ordered steaks, baked potatoes and salads. He stared into the flickering flame of the candle in the center of the table, then slowly raised his eyes to look at Megan.

"A police officer, a detective named Rick, was killed last night," he said, his voice hushed. "He was a decent man, and he's dead."

"I'm sorry, Steel," Megan said quietly. "No wonder you're so tense, upset. It has to be very difficult for you when this happens."

"Megan, it could have been me instead of Rick."

"Or Casey, or any one of a hundred others."

"Aren't you listening to me? I could be in the morgue right now."

"Are you trying to frighten me, Steel?"

"I'm trying to get you to face facts. What's the point of planning a future with someone if—"

"If they might die tomorrow? Steel, that element is in everyone's lives. People are killed crossing the street on their way to a nice safe job like selling insurance."

"Police officers court death, taunt it, dare it to pick them next. It's a game of roulette, and eventually someone loses."

"And some don't. What are you saying to me, Steel?"

"I don't know. This is the first time I've ever looked further than the man himself who was cut down. Now I'm seeing the whole picture: his wife, baby, or an empty space because he had neither. It's confusing as hell. Casey and his wife are thinking about having another baby and he doesn't even know if he'll be alive to see that kid born. That's not fair to Sally. Casey has some reponsibility here."

"To do what? Force his family to live in constant fear? What kind of life would that be?"

"Realistic."

"Realistic? Oh, Steel, come on. No one can exist in a state of impending doom. You've been a policeman for a long time. You've learned to live with the dangers and unknowns. I realize you're upset about Rick, but surely you've faced this type of tragedy before."

"Yeah," he said, raking his hand through his hair, "when I was alone. I love you, Megan, and suddenly there's a new slant to the whole scenario. I'm questioning my right to bring you into the world I chose to exist in."

"Don't I have the right to an opinion?"

"I'm not sure. I have to be able to live with my conscience. Look, let's drop it for now. I've been over it so many times, my brain is turning into mush. Let's just relax and enjoy ourselves. I have to make a phone call and then no more heavy talk. I'll be right back."

"All right, Steel," Megan said, forcing a smile. Relax and enjoy? she thought. When her future with Steel was hanging by a slender thread? When her newfound happiness was a breath away from being crushed into dust and whisked into oblivion? Steel was waging an inner war, a battle of his conscience versus his love for her. He might look deep within himself and decide he had no choice but to protect her from possible pain by walking away from her and their love. No! Oh, no, he couldn't. Didn't he realize that no risk was too great if it meant being with him? She'd accepted his career and all that went with it. Why couldn't he see that? "Oh, Steel," she whispered, "don't leave me. Please don't do this to us."

Steel drummed his fingers impatiently on the metal box housing the telephone as he heard the ringing on the other end. Casey finally answered.

"Jones."

"Steel. I'll make it quick."

"Don't you ever go off duty?"

"Yeah, I'm having dinner with Megan right now."

"No, you're not, you're talking to me."

"Two seconds, Casey, that's all I need."

"I'm timing you. Speak."

"Diamonds. Or rubies, sapphires, whatever. Valuable gems, Casey."

"What about them?"

"It's a far-out hunch. Can you contact that Fed who's supposed to cooperate with us and see if there's been an international jewel heist where the stuff never surfaced?"

"Yeah, I suppose, but why?"

"I'm not sure yet. I'm trying to put all the pieces together in my mind. The Bureau boy hopefully had enough sense to pick up brochures at every place Bodeen took pictures in Paris. Tell him we want those pamphlets."

"Got it. Why?"

"Gut feeling, Casey, and I could be out in left field. I'd better get back to Megan, so I'll fill you in later."

"On Monday, not sooner. We need a break, Steel. Have Megan tell Clara to run the store over the weekend. Nothing can happen until Frank Sands contacts Megan anyway, and she just won't be available."

"Okay."

"Spend a couple days with your lady, Steel. You two deserve it."

"Yeah, you're right. I'll see you Monday."

"Just concentrate on Megan for the next two days. Think you can handle the assignment?"

"No sweat."

"Take her to Vegas and get married, you fool!"

"Bye, Jones," Steel said, laughing as he hung up. Concentrate on Megan for the next two days, he thought. Man, that sounded great. First thing he'd better do is go apologize for the rotten mood he'd been in when he'd picked her up. He'd come on pretty strong about Rick.

Megan stiffened as she watched Steel make his way across the room to their table, and she clutched her trembling hands tightly in her lap.

He moves with such pantherlike grace, she thought, such an aura of power. Oh, how she loved him, needed him. Was he going to leave her? Oh, dear heaven, was he?

Steel settled into his chair and placed his hand palm up on the table. Megan looked at him questioningly, then lifted her hand to place it in his. He stared at her slender fingers and then stroked them gently with his thumb before raising his dark eyes once more to gaze at her warmly.

"I'm sorry, Megan," he said. "I shouldn't have jumped all over you like I did. Would you consider going away with me for the weekend? Just the two of us. Clara can run the store and we won't give a moment's thought to Bodeen. What do you say?"

"Oh, Steel, yes!" Megan said, smiling, a rush of joy and relief sweeping through her. "That sounds wonderful."

"Great. Here's our dinner. After we eat, you call Clara. Let's hope she's home on a Friday night. If not, we'll catch her in the morning."

"Anything else for you folks?" the waitress asked.

"Everything is perfect," Megan said, a lovely smile on her face.

Incredible, Steel thought. Had he done that? Brought that beautiful smile to her face? He knew he possessed the power to shatter her by losing his life in the line of duty, but was he capable of bringing her this much joy?

Him? Blade of Steel Danner could make her green eyes sparkle like that? Love was really something.

Steel could feel the tension ebbing from his body as they ate. Megan asked him endless questions about his childhood on the Hopi Indian reservation in Arizona, and he told her how he and Roddy had been raised by their grandfather, Chief Hawk in Hand Danner, after the death of their parents in an automobile accident. Their mother had been a missionary assigned to the Hopi reservation in northern Arizona, where she had met, fallen in love with and married the chief's son, Strong of Heart Danner.

Megan then spoke of Mrs. Turnbull, of the gracious, loving woman who had changed the course of her life. It was a sharing time, a special time, a loving time, as they talked on in the glow of the candlelight.

"We'd better go," Steel said finally, "before they start charging us rent for this table."

"It's been a lovely evening."

"It isn't over," he said, pushing himself to his feet.

Megan smiled and rose to join him, welcoming the strength of his arm, which encircled her shoulders. Outside, the air was cool, the sky an umbrella of stars overhead, as Steel assisted Megan into the car, then walked around to slide behind the wheel.

"Okay, let's get organized," he said, turning the key in the ignition. "We'll go pick up your car, I'll follow you to your place, you call Clara, then pack. We'll stay at my place tonight and get an early start in the morning."

"You'll have to tell me where we're going so I'll know what to take."

"Jeans and sweaters, sweaters and jeans. We're going to a rustic little cabin where there's no telephone."

"Marvelous. Who owns it?"

"I do."

When they reached her apartment, Megan snatched up the receiver to the telephone and quickly dialed Clara's number. To Megan's delight, Clara was indeed at home and cheerfully agreed to run Memory Lane over the weekend. Steel called the man who ran the general store near the cabin and asked him to air out the cabin and stock it with enough food for two for the weekend.

A short time later in Steel's living room, he flicked on the light, set Megan's suitcase on the floor and turned to her, closing the door by reaching over her head. She leaned back against the wooden panel as he braced his large hands flat on the door on either side of her head and smiled down at her.

"Hello, my Megan," he said softly, and then lowered his head to brush his lips across hers.

Megan kept her arms at her sides as Steel's lips trailed a ribbon of kisses over her face and down the slender column of her neck. He kept his body away, not touching, and the anticipation of reaching for him caused her knees to tremble. His tongue drew a lazy circle around her lips and then parted them; flickering, dipping, dueling with hers. The heat emanating from Steel's rugged frame seemed to cover her in a cloak of warmth that heightened her passion as she moaned deep within her throat.

Steel inched his hands closer, his long fingers finally weaving into her satiny hair as the pressure of his mouth increased. In a languorous journey his hands stroked her cheeks, throat, the slope of her shoulders, coming to rest at the sides of her breasts. Megan's arms felt heavy, leaden, as she lifted them upward to circle Steel's neck and inch her fingers into the night darkness of his hair.

And then at last, *at last*, he gathered her into his tight embrace, lifting his head to draw a labored breath, then taking possession of her mouth again. Their raspy breathing echoed in the quiet room as Steel pressed Megan to him, fitting her into the sharp contours of his body, his manhood strong against her.

"Oh, Steel," Megan gasped, going nearly limp in his arms.

"I will never get enough of you," he grated, his voice hoarse with desire. "I love you, Megan. I want you so much."

"Yes," she said, and walked with him across the room to the bedroom.

Their lovemaking was urgent, frenzied, as their kindled passions raged out of control. Clothes were shed and they came together without speaking. With mutual need and understanding, they reached for each other and became one. Their rhythmic motions were synchronized, thundering, creating a tempo for the dance of lovers that burst into rainbow colors at the crescendo. Heartbeats drummed the cadence, and names called aloud were the litany.

"Steel!"

"Yes, Megan, yes!"

Clinging together they drifted back as bodies cooled and breathing returned to normal levels. Steel moved away and pulled Megan to his side, resting his lips on her forehead. They softly declared their love and then they slept, with Megan's hand covering the silver hawk on Steel's chest.

They left early the next morning and were soon leaving the smog-laden city behind as Steel drove up the coast. They stopped for breakfast at a small café and started out again, chatting comfortably, falling silent, then talking again. Megan leaned her head against the headrest of the seat and closed her eyes.

"Sleepy?" Steel asked.

"No, just very contented. I never dreamed I could be this happy, Steel. You've brought so much joy into my life."

"I'm glad," he said. And he could bring her so much pain. He frowned. No, he wouldn't think about that. Not now. Not during these stolen hours. He was there, alive, with Megan, and that's all that mattered.

Steel worked his way off the main highway and wove through the narrow roads edged by towering trees. Just under three hours after leaving Los Angeles, he drove down a bumpy dirt path and stopped next to a small cabin.

"Home away from home," he said, turning off the ignition.

"Oh!" Megan said, hurrying out of the car. "It's darling! Just like a real log cabin. Listen to the birds! Oh, I hope we see some squirrels and rabbits. Are there deer up here? A chimney! Can we have a fire in the hearth? Oh, hurry, Steel, I want to see the inside."

Steel chuckled and shook his head as he followed Megan to the front door of the cabin. She was like an excited little girl, he thought. Her eyes were dancing and her cheeks were flushed. She'd never known happiness as a child, and he was going to make it up to her. All of it. He'd fill her days with laughter and her nights with the exquisite lovemaking they shared. She could drop her pennies in the fountain, and he'd do everything humanly possible to see that her wishes came true. He loved her.

"Oh, Steel," Megan whispered as he unlocked the door and pushed it open, "it's lovely."

Megan moved slowly forward, her eyes sweeping over the rustic room. There was a stone fireplace with a heavy wooden mantel and a braided rug in front on the hardwood floor. Early American furniture was homey and appealing, and in the corner of the room sat a huge old-fashioned brass bed covered with a patchwork quilt. A small kitchen in the back held table and chairs, and a bathroom was off the kitchen. It was warm and welcoming, and Megan was smiling when she moved into Steel's embrace.

"It's perfect," she said, looking up at him. "So charming and cozy. Thank you for bringing me."

"I've never brought a woman here before, Megan. I've come alone, or Casey has tagged along when we needed to unwind, but that's about all. There's never been anyone else I've wanted to share it with."

"I feel very special, very loved."

"You are," he said, claiming her mouth in a long, searing kiss. "Now," he said, when he finally released her, "I'm hungry."

"Figures," she said, laughing. "I'll scout out the kitchen."

"I'll bring in the suitcases. We'll eat and then go for a walk in the woods. Okay?"

"Okay!"

It was heavenly. They walked hand in hand through the thick trees, collected pinecones and stopped often to share a lengthy kiss. Megan laughed in delight when she saw squirrels and rabbits, and Steel seemed to have a continual smile on his face as he watched her. There was no world beyond the two of them. There was only Megan and Steel. Together.

With the dusk came crisp, cold air, and Steel made a roaring fire in the hearth. In the warmth of the leaping flames they consumed enormous ham sandwiches and sipped mugs of steaming tomato soup. Darkness fell over the peaceful woods, and Megan snuggled close to Steel on the sofa, the fire casting a soothing glow over the cabin.

"What a wonderful day," Megan said softly.

"Yes, it was. I'm glad you're here, Megan. I've enjoyed it when I've come alone, but never like today. I love to hear your laughter in this room, in the woods. You deserve to be happy. I only hope that I...well..."

"*You* are my happiness, Steel. You and I together. I love you so very, very much."

"But what if...no, I won't start in on the gloom-and-doom stuff. Today, tomorrow, are just for us as if no one else, or nowhere else, exists."

"Perfect."

They made sweet, slow, sensuous love in the old-fashioned bed then, as the fire in the hearth burned down to glowing coals, they slept, entwined in each other's arms.

The next day, they walked in another direction and found a running stream with crystal-clear water. They made tiny boats out of leaves and twigs and had a race, cheering on the crafts that floated along as Megan and Steel ran along the edge. Steel's boat won when Megan's capsized, and she yelled foul, claiming Indians had an inside edge on building canoes.

"Five o'clock," Steel said, back at the cabin as they consumed huge bowls of hot stew. "We'd better pack up and start home."

"I hate to leave."

"We can come again."

"I'd like that."

"Once we get this business with Bodeen wrapped up, we'll take a few days off."

"You want to put him in jail very badly, don't you?"

"Yeah, I really do. He's a lowlife who's destroyed so many lives, including kids, because of his drug ring. Bodeen is... Can you understand why I don't want you at Memory Lane?"

"Yes, I understand, but I won't change my mind. I'm staying at my store."

"Yeah, well, I hope Frank Sands contacts you soon so we can get the show on the road. I want this thing finished and your involvement in it ended as quickly as possible."

"I know. So do I."

"Well, back to reality. Let's go home."

The drive back to Los Angeles was quiet and pleasant. The time seemed to pass too quickly and before long they were back at Megan's apartment. In the living room, before he left to go home, Steel pulled her into his arms and kissed her deeply.

"I love you," he said. "The weekend was perfect because we were together. I'll talk to you tomorrow."

"All right. I love you, Blade of Steel."

In his own apartment, Steel took a can of beer from the refrigerator, yanked off the tab and walked into the living room. He sat down on the sofa, got up again and then settled once more on the cushion with a sigh and a deep frown.

He missed Megan, he thought. He'd just left her and he already missed her! The apartment was too empty, too quiet. "Ah, hell," he said, taking several swallows of beer. "I sound like a kid with a crush on a cheer-leader." No, he thought, he was a man in love with a woman. He wanted the whole package: a wife, a son, a...goldfish in a bowl with pretty marbles in the bottom. Other men who carried guns as a part of their life's work had it all. Casey did, so why shouldn't he? "Because I can't promise to stay alive," he said to the empty room. "Maybe Casey can handle that but I don't know if I can. I don't want Megan to be left all alone."

Steel slept restlessly that night, waking often, and reaching for Megan. But she wasn't there.

The office was empty when Steel arrived the next morning. He sank into his chair and stared moodily at the far wall.

A line of perspiration broke out on his forehead and another trickled down his back as he thought once again of Rick. The man was dead. If there had been a woman she would be alone. At home there might have been a baby who would never even remember its father. What was the purpose of it all? What sense was there in loving, dreaming of the future, making plans and creating a child? In a breath of a moment, one squeeze of a trigger or slash of a knife, it was over, the dreams shattered, replaced by tears and emptiness. What gave any of them wearing guns and badges the right to love?

"Hi, y'all," Casey said, coming into the room and snapping Steel out of his reverie. "Have a good weekend?"

"What? Oh, yeah, great. I took Megan to the cabin. We had a really nice time. Did you talk to that Fed?"

"Yep, he's got the brochures from every place Bodeen took pictures in Paris and will send them over by messenger. What's this wild idea of yours?"

"I'm still trying to piece it together. Smuggling junk into the country in antiques is out, right?"

"I'd say so. Customs and the Bureau are one step ahead of all that now. That stuff comes in clean as a whistle."

"But what about when it goes back out?"

"What do you mean? Every country has customs, Steel."

"Yeah, but we're missing something—some clue. I need to check on something with Megan, then I'll know how far off the track I am."

"You're probably blowing smoke, pal," Casey said.

"Probably."

"Well, one thing's for sure, Steel. Whatever Bodeen's into it's big. Very big."

"And Megan's right in the middle of it," Steel said tightly. "Right in the damn middle."

Nine

Steel left the office and returned with a quart of milk from the kitchen.

"What's the word on international jewels being heisted and never fenced?" he said, sinking into his chair.

"Zip. The Fed said to look closer to home. Princess Somebody had her jewelry lifted two years ago in New York City. And listen to this. At the time, there were underground rumblings that it was Bodeen's deal, but according to the fine fences who know about these things, none of it ever surfaced."

"How much was it worth?"

"About two million, give or take a hundred grand or so."

Steel whistled long and low. "Nice day's work," he said, nodding. "Frankie baby could buy a lot of cigars with those kind of bucks. Let me check something out with Megan," he said, picking up the receiver to the telephone.

"Memory Lane," Megan said, a few moments later.

"Hi, babe," Steel said, an instant smile on his face. Casey chuckled and shook his head. "Clara around?"

"No, she isn't in yet this morning."

"Good. Megan, when antiques are brought into this country and clear customs is there paperwork to that effect? Do the people handling the auction get documents saying the stuff is clean?"

"Yes, they do."

"Okay, now suppose someone buys something here and decides to ship it back out of the country?"

"They have a choice. They can go through customs again, or have the auctioning house seal the item in a crate in a prescribed manner that alleviates the need to have another inspection made."

"Aw right!" Steel said, smacking his hand on the desk. "That's exactly what I wanted to hear."

"That's nice," Megan said, laughing. "Am I wonderful?"

"You're fantastic! I'll talk to you later."

"I thought I'd cook dinner for you tonight at my place."

"You're on," he said. "I'll see you there. Bye."

"So? What's the scoop?" Casey demanded as Steel hung up. "You look awfully pleased with yourself, Blade of Steel. There's nothing worse than a smug Indian."

"Antiques clear customs and the auctioning house gets papers saying so. If the buyer wants to ship it back overseas, he can hassle with the red tape again or—get this, Casey—or have the item crated in a special way by the outfit who sold it and take it on out, skipping customs. No fuss, no muss.''

"Go on," Casey said thoughtfully, nodding his head.

"Bodeen goes to Paris and sees what Megan bought to be shipped over here. He takes a picture of it, along with others as a smoke screen. He comes home with a very detailed snapshot of the piece Megan bought. Now he has to convince Megan to sell it to *him*, instead of her original client. He has the crate properly sealed for shipping back out of the country, and then—''

"Pulls a switch!" Casey said, jumping to his feet.

"Bingo! He's had that piece duplicated here, and it's chock full of two million dollars worth of jewels. Even if an overcautious customs man decides to take a peek, the item is exactly what appears on the documents.''

"But what about this fancy sealing job?''

"Come on, Casey. Bodeen isn't going to let something like that stop him. You'd better believe he'll know how to get into that crate and reseal it as though it's never been touched.''

"This is all a long shot, Steel, but, hell, it fits together like a charm. Man, what a slick operation. So what did Megan buy over in Paris?''

"That's why I wanted to look at those brochures the Fed got. Megan got a mirror, but I wanted to see for myself that it would work.''

"I'll go check with Ginger and see if the messenger service brought anything over," Casey said, heading for the door.

A few minutes later, Casey returned with a large brown envelope.

"Got 'em?" Steel asked.

"Yep. Here, you take half," Casey said, then settled into his chair. "Boy, this stuff is gross. People pay big bucks for this?"

"Yeah. We are looking, by the way, for a framed mirror from the estate of Henri DuPont."

"Huh?"

"Have you no culture? There is a vast market for show biz memorabilia."

"And you, of course, know all about these things."

"Of course. Look at the pictures. I can't help it if you have no social graces like knowing the intricacies of the antique business."

"You're so full of bull, Danner," Casey said, laughing.

"Look at the pictures, Jones. I'm not positive that Bodeen would use this cruddy mirror, but the way Megan described it, it would work. Of course, I don't know that he has those gems, either."

"You sure don't know much," Casey muttered. "Hey, here's a spittoon. It looks like a potty chair."

"What's next?" Captain Meredith said, coming into the room. "After picture books, you take up finger painting?"

"Yep," Steel said, concentrating on the brochure.

"You any closer to breaking open this thing with Bodeen?" the captain asked.

"Here it is!" Steel said, getting to his feet. "Henri DuPont's mirror."

"Steel is ever so very knowledgeable about antiques, Captain," Casey said. "It's awesome."

"Okay, let's see," Steel said. "Aw right! It's being cleared through the House of Sawyer in two weeks, having been purchased by Memory Lane. They must update these brochures every couple of days. Ten bucks says Bodeen wanted that mirror, found out that Megan bought it before he could get his hands on it, and then decided to set up the whole scam at Memory Lane. I'm telling you, it all fits together. I am either a genius, or I'm so wrong about the whole bit it's a sin.''

"Wanna vote on that one?" Captain Meredith said. "I think I'll leave you to your insanity. But, gentlemen, get Bodeen. I'm going to bury a good cop. Bodeen wasn't involved in Rick's death, but maybe I'd feel better if we put a louse like Frankie behind bars. I want Bodeen's butt.''

"We all do," Steel said. "This time he's going to pay up.''

Captain Meredith nodded and then walked to the door, stopping with his back to the two men. "Get Bodeen," he said, then left the room.

Steel sank back into his chair and stared at the door Captain Meredith had closed behind him. He felt as though he had been kicked in the stomach, the pain causing a momentary roaring in his ears.

"Steel?" Casey said. "What's wrong?"

"It could have been any of us, Casey. Maybe Rick did the playboy bit on purpose because he knew he could be wiped out at any moment. It could be that he didn't allow himself a serious commitment because he didn't know how long he'd be alive.''

"Come on, Steel. We all expect to be alive."

"Do we, Casey? Can you promise Sally you'll be here when that new baby of yours is born? Did you think about that when you got her pregnant?''

"Think about dying when I'm making love to my wife? When I'm hopefully creating a child within her? Hell, no! That's sick, Steel. What's with you? You accepted the dangers of this job years ago. Now you're insinuating I have no sense of decency because I'm bringing my children into the world? What in the hell has happened to you?"

"I was alone then! I had no one to answer to but myself!"

"Ah, man," Casey said, slouching back in his chair, "it's Megan."

"Damn right, it's Megan!" Steel said, a pulse beating in the strong column of his neck. "What gives me the right to drag her into this mess? When I leave her I can't promise I'll be back. I can't!"

"Neither can the mailman! Damn it, Steel, you said Megan accepted what you do for a living. She's not asking for guarantees any more than my Sally is. What are we supposed to do? Go to bed with our guns, be cops twenty-four hours a day? Not have a wife, family, hopes and dreams for the future? We're men, not robots. We do our jobs to the best of our ability and then go home to the people who love us. You've got this all twisted around in your head."

"Do I? Maybe I'm the only one seeing it clearly. I have the ability to make Megan smile, laugh right out loud. She deserves that. It's her turn to be happy and, believe it or not, I can do that for her. But, Casey, I am also the one who could shatter her into a million pieces. If I get killed she's going to cry. I don't want to make her cry, Casey."

"Don't do it, Steel," Casey said. "Don't throw away a lifetime with Megan over a maybe. Maybe you'll get cut down, but the odds say you won't. You're in love for the first time in your life. Hang on to that love, Steel. Marry your lady, have the son you want to give the silver hawk to. Live each day as it comes and count your blessings. You have that right. We all do."

"I don't know," Steel said, his head sinking into his hands. "I just . . . don't know."

In the late afternoon, Megan reached absently for the ringing telephone as she studied a brochure.

"Memory Lane."

"Miss James?"

"Yes."

"Frank Sands. How are you, my dear?"

Megan gripped the receiver so tightly her knuckles turned white from the pressure. Her heart was racing, and she prayed to the heavens that her voice was steady when she spoke.

"Very well, thank you. And you?" she asked, pressing her hand to her forehead.

"Splendid. My wife has at last decided on what she wants for her gift."

"Oh?"

"A charming little mirror from the estate of Henri DuPont that you purchased in Paris and are clearing through the House of Sawyer in two weeks."

"But—" Megan began. That was Mrs. Morrison's mirror! Oh, dear heaven, now what was she going to do? "Of course, Mr. Sands, I'd be glad to sell you the mirror. It's a darling piece. It will be three thousand dollars, plus the cost of my trip to Paris." That ought to stop him, she decided smugly. He'd surely pick something instead of the mirror now.

"Excellent," he said.

Damn it! Megan thought. "Fine," she said, gritting her teeth.

"Oh, just one other little thing, Miss James. I plan to take my wife to Greece, and as a surprise, I want to give her the mirror once we arrive. Therefore, I'll need the item packed, sealed and documented for customs.''

''I'll have the House of Sawyer take care of it. Are you coming here to Memory Lane to pick it up?''

''We'll discuss that part later. I'll call you after you get the mirror. Goodbye, Miss James.''

''Goodbye, Mr. Sands.''

Megan replaced the receiver and leaned back in her chair, closing her eyes as she drew a steadying breath. She had to call Steel, she thought. She had to tell him that Frank Sands . . . that Bodeen . . . had just contacted her about the Henri DuPont mirror. She couldn't sell that mirror to him! She'd given her word to Mrs. Morrison, and the reputation of Memory Lane was at stake!

''Are you all right, Megan?'' Clara asked from the doorway.

''What? Oh, yes, of course. Why don't you go ahead and unpack those saltcellars that came in?''

''Sure thing.''

Megan chewed on her bottom lip after Clara returned to the front of the store. She didn't dare risk calling Steel while Clara was there, she thought. And if she suddenly decided to go out, Clara might report it to Frankie Bodeen. She had no choice but to stay put, act naturally and wait to tell Steel what had transpired when he arrived at her apartment for dinner. In the meantime, she would try desperately not to have a nervous breakdown! Oh, this cops and robbers stuff was the pits!

Steel and Casey spent the remainder of the afternoon working on a cat burglar case with two other detectives. The four went over stacks of old files in the hope of finding someone who operated with the strange habit of scrawling a message on the victim's wall with lipstick. It was tedious, but necessary, and Steel and Casey had volunteered their time.

"Nada," Casey said. "This joker dumped perfume on bedspreads, but he's doing five to ten. Looks like you guys might have a rookie."

"Wonderful," the detective muttered. "Doesn't anyone believe in honest labor these days? Hey, it's late. I've got to get home. My wife is rattled because of Rick and she'll be watching the clock."

"She's upset?" Steel said.

"Well, sure. I imagine all the wives are. I just try to show up on time or call her until things get back to normal."

"What's normal?" Steel asked. "Her wondering if you're next every time you leave the house?"

"Oh, brother, here he goes," Casey said, rolling his eyes.

"No," the man said, "she doesn't. If it happens, she'll deal with it. We can't wear danger like a hair shirt, Steel."

"Amen," Casey said.

"Night," the man said. "Thanks for the help, guys."

"Yeah," Casey said as the pair left the room. "You're getting to be a pain in the butt, Steel."

"Me? Why?"

"You're on a soapbox about this cops-being-family-men bit."

"You're right, and I'm sorry, Casey. It's my problem and I shouldn't be dumping on everyone."

"Hey, you talk, I'll listen, but I'm afraid that ultimately it has to be your decision. I just hope you make the right one."

"And you know what that is, of course."

"Yep. See you tomorrow," Casey said, punching Steel on the arm and then leaving the room.

"See ya," Steel said, staring at a spot on the wall. Where was he going to find the answers? he thought. When he was with Megan, she was all that mattered; but when he stepped away, the questions of right and wrong screamed in his mind. He wanted to marry her. He honestly did. But he couldn't get a handle on the battle he was fighting in his mind. "Ah, hell," he muttered, pushing himself to his feet and leaving the office.

Steel drove home, showered and changed into jeans and a navy-blue sweater. As he combed his hair in front of the bathroom mirror, he frowned at his reflection.

"Hello, Lieutenant," he said, "how's life? Screwed up? Yes. I hear you're in love. How nice. So, why aren't you married instead of sprucing up for a date like a teenager? Oh? You're confused, not sure if marriage mixes with cops and guns?"

Steel strode out of the bathroom, walked through the bedroom and living room and left the apartment, closing the door behind him with a reverberating thud.

He couldn't go on like this, Steel decided as he drove to Megan's. It was the indecision that was driving him nuts. He was a detective. A damn good detective. He gathered the facts, put them together like a jigsaw puzzle and came to a conclusion. He also relied on his gut instinct, listened to that little inner voice that pointed him in the right direction. So, why couldn't he do that on the subject of Megan and marriage, babies and diapers? He could, and he would!

"Okay, so do it," he said to the rearview mirror. He loved her. She loved him, he thought. He wanted a son to give the silver hawk to. Did Megan want children? Hell, yes, she even wanted a goldfish in a pretty bowl with marbles on the bottom. He was a cop. She accepted that, no questions asked. He wanted to marry his Megan. "Well, Blade of Steel?" he asked. "What's the verdict?"

Steel pulled into the parking lot at Megan's apartment, turned off the ignition and sat as still as a statue. And then he waited. He waited for his inner voice to speak, to give him the answer he so desperately sought.

But from deep within himself, from the very recesses of his soul, there was only a chilling silence.

Ten

Megan straightened her green sweater over the waist-band of her jeans, then pinched her cheeks as she examined her reflection in the mirror. The hours since Frank Sands had telephoned her at Memory Lane had been an agonizingly slow passing of time. Her forced smile and relaxed demeanor for customers, and especially for Clara, had been more and more difficult to maintain. With a grateful sigh, Megan had bid Clara good-night, closed the store and driven home to her apartment.

Now with chicken and potatoes baking in the oven, the table set for two and wine waiting to be uncorked, Megan needed only one more addition to calm her jangled nerves: Blade of Steel Danner. She had fanciful images of him arriving in full Indian headdress with bow and arrow in hand, ready to rescue her from the evil clutches of Frankie Bodeen. Steel would let out an ear splitting war cry and . . .

"You're getting crazy, Megan," she said to her image in the mirror, and marched from the bedroom just as a knock sounded at the door.

"Hi, babe," Steel said, when Megan flung open the door. "I hope I'm not later than you—"

Steel's words were cut off as Megan grabbed him by the arm and hauled him into the room. She poked her head out into the hall, looked up and down the corridor, then slammed the door and flattened herself against the wooden panel.

"Hi!" she said brightly. "You're here."

"Right," he said, nodding as he squinted at her warily. "Megan! What is your problem? Are you permanently attached to that door, or could I pry you loose and kiss you hello?"

"Oh, Steel," she said, flinging herself at his chest and being caught by strong, comforting arms. "He called. Frank Sands called me. It was too risky to contact you or leave the store, so I've been waiting and waiting to see you—"

"Easy, babe. Let's sit down," he said, leading her to the sofa and pulling her down next to him. "Now, nice and slow. What did Bodeen say?"

"Well, he said, 'How are you, my dear?'"

"Oh," Steel chuckled, kissing her on the forehead. "We don't have to get quite so technical here. We'll skip over the greetings and go straight to the nitty-gritty. Did he tell you what he wanted you to get for him?"

"The mirror from Henri DuPont's estate that I bought in Paris for Mrs. Morrison. It's clearing through the House of Sawyer in two weeks."

Steel stiffened, every muscle in his body tightening as he heard Megan's words. This is it! he thought. Right on the money! They had him. They were going to get Frankie Bodeen!

"Steel, your eyes have gone all cold. Please don't slip away from me. Not now. I need you here, really here with me."

"I'm not going anywhere," he growled, cupping her face in his hands and taking possession of her mouth in a hard, searing kiss.

Megan's tension and fear were instantly replaced by euphoria as she returned Steel's kiss in total abandonment. Everything was fine now, she thought dreamily. Everything was under control because Steel was there. He loved her, would protect and care for her. With that knowledge she could take on anything and anyone, Frankie Bodeen included.

"Is that how you calm down all your witnesses?" she said breathlessly, when Steel lifted his head.

"Sure. Works wonders. Are you all right?"

"Yes, I'm fine now. All those hours waiting to see you just took their toll on my nerves. Steel, Bodeen wants the mirror sealed at the auctioning house so he can take it to Greece as a surprise for his wife."

"Exactly right. Did he say when and where he'd pick it up?"

"No, he said he'd talk to me after I had the mirror, so I assume I'm to bring it back to Memory Lane."

"Then that's the only piece of the puzzle missing. Will he risk taking it somewhere and pulling the switch, or do it right at the store so he has the mirror in his possession as little as possible?"

"Switch?"

"A fake mirror, Megan. One he had made up from the pictures he took in Paris and loaded with two million dollars in stolen gems."

"Good heavens," she whispered.

"He'll switch the mirrors, reseal the crate to perfection and walk out of this country and into another one with no questions asked."

"Not a bad caper," Megan said nodding. "Thing is, he can't have that mirror."

"What?"

"It belongs to Mrs. Morrison."

"You didn't tell Bodeen that, did you?" Steel asked, frowning deeply.

"Well, no, but I have no intention of breaking my word to a client."

"Damn it, Megan, quit messing around. Bodeen has to get the mirror, and you know it. Tell your weird old lady to pick something else."

"We're talking about the reputation of my store!"

"No!" he roared. "We're talking about finally catching a bastard!"

"Oh," she said softly. "I guess I've been on my own so long, worked so hard by myself, that I forgot what teamwork is all about. We're partners, you and I, in everything, aren't we? This is a new role for me. I'm sorry, Steel. Of course, I'll sell the mirror to Bodeen."

"Being half of a whole is new for me, too, Megan," he said gently. "We're learning, together. I've got to call Casey."

"Okay, I'll check on dinner."

"Megan, it's still not too late for you to pull out. We could put someone in your place."

"No, Steel, I'm staying. I know I was a basket case when you arrived, but I won't let you down, I promise."

"Bodeen won't touch you. I'll be there, close. You simply follow his instructions and leave the rest to me and Casey. But, damn, I don't want you involved in this!"

"Tough tomatoes, Lieutenant," she said, getting to her feet and tilting her nose in the air. "I am a vital member of this team, and you're stuck with me. I will now go check my chicken."

"Tough tomatoes?" Steel muttered, reaching for the telephone. "Who's she been hanging out with?"

Casey whooped his approval at Steel's news and went so far as to say that Indians had superior minds on limited occasions.

"How's Megan holding up?" Casey asked.

"She's fine. She was a little shook up when I got here, but now she's back to normal. Casey, I don't want anything to happen to her."

"She won't be hurt, Steel. She's just the messenger and Bodeen can't possibly think otherwise. Clara has been watching Megan, remember? We'll work out a plan to cover Megan like super glue. We've got two weeks to fine-tune this thing. Nothing is going to go wrong. Nothing, Steel."

"Yeah, okay. I'll see you in the morning."

"If I know you, you're tight as a drum. Relax. Megan will sense it if you're tense, worried. Just have a pleasant evening and night. Understand?"

"Oh, stuff it, Jones," Steel said, laughing.

"Nighty night, Danner."

Steel replaced the receiver and watched as Megan brought dishes of food to the small table in the dining area at the end of the living room. His heart thundered in his chest, and he had the irrational urge to snatch her up and take her back to the cabin in the woods. Take her away to someplace safe where he could protect her from Frankie Bodeen. Fine-tune it, Casey had said. Hell, they were going over every detail a thousand times to ensure Megan's safety. A million times if need be!

"Dinner is served," Megan said. "Will you open the wine, Steel?"

"What?"

"The wine."

"Oh, sure," he said, pushing himself to his feet and walking to the table. "Looks good, smells good."

"Me, or the food?"

"Both."

"Sit and enjoy."

Steel opened the wine and filled their glasses, then sat down opposite Megan at the table, raising his glass in a toast.

"Here's to pennies in the fountain. Your pennies, your fountain, your wishes," he said. "May they all come true."

"Thank you," she said, smiling as she clicked glasses with him and took a sip of the wine. "I hope your wishes come true, too, Steel."

"Well, we don't want to wear out the fountain. It probably has a set number of wishes it grants per year."

"Magic fountains? Heavens, no. They grant wishes forever. What did Casey say?"

"He figures we'll get Bodeen this time for sure. Look, if you want to talk about it some more we will, or we can give it a rest for tonight. Whatever will make you the most comfortable is fine with me. You're the important person here, Megan."

"Thank you, Steel. That was a lovely thing to say."

"Megan, I love you. I'd give anything if you weren't involved in this. Do you want to discuss it for a while?"

"No, I don't think so. Not now, anyway. Let's eat before this gets cold."

"Megan, if you had a baby..."

"I beg your pardon?" she said, her fork stopping in midair.

"Humor me. What would you do about Memory Lane if you had a baby?"

"Hire a manager. Then I'd drop in when it suited me and probably attend the auctions myself. That's one of the nice parts of having your own business. You make it adjust to your needs."

"You'd want to be home most of the time with your child?"

"Oh, yes. I want two children or maybe even three, so my home is ringing with laughter. Even my goldfish would have a smile on its face."

"Fish don't smile."

"Mine would."

"Yeah, it probably would, because you're a sunshine gal. This is a delicious dinner. You have many talents, my love."

"Oh?"

"We'll discuss the others later."

"Discuss?"

"More like show-and-tell."

"Splendid," Megan said, smiling.

They ate in silence for several minutes, and Megan beamed when Steel refilled his plate. She brought steaming cups of coffee to the table and a plate of fruit and cheese for dessert.

"You're spoiling me," Steel said. "You really are."

"And I'm having a marvelous time doing it."

"Megan, I think I should tell you something."

"All right."

"For the first time in my life I have a wish, a reason to drop a penny in the fountain. *You* are my wish. I...want to marry you, share in the birth of our children and spend the rest of my life with you. But there, right there, is the problem. Part of my life includes being a cop. I can't get a handle on bringing a wife and baby into such a risky existence. I don't know what to do."

"I see," Megan said softly. "I guess all I can say is that I love you and I want to be your wife and bear your children more than any other wish I've ever had. But, Steel, unless you find an inner peace about this, it isn't going to work. You would be torn in two every time you went on duty and you couldn't survive that way. Everything will have to fall into its proper place for you before you could marry me and still be a good detective."

"I know that."

"I will marry you, Steel Danner, with pride and love on the day you know in your heart and soul that it's the right thing for you. Because if it isn't, we'll never be truly happy. You owe it to both of us to be very, very sure. I'll wait for you, Steel. Take all the time you need."

"I don't deserve you, Megan. You're so special, rare."

"So are you, Blade of Steel. I think I'll have another glass of wine. It's not every day in a girl's life she almost gets proposed to."

"I think I'm a louse," Steel said, frowning.

"I think you're wonderful."

Their eyes met and held in a long, tender gaze as neither spoke. Steel covered Megan's hand with his and stroked it gently with his thumb. Time lost meaning as they simply looked at each other.

"Oh, Lord!" Megan shrieked as the ringing of the telephone shattered the silence and the mood. "I'll get it. Goodness, it scared the socks off me. Hello," she said, snatching up the receiver.

"Megan? Hi, this is Roddy Clark, Steel's sister. Casey gave me your number."

"Oh, of course."

"I'm sorry to disturb you, but I thought Steel would like to know I'm on the way to the hospital to have my baby."

"What? You're what?"

"My water broke and it looks like tonight is the night."

"Steel, Roddy is having her baby!"

"Now?" he said, scrambling to his feet and striding to the telephone. "Roddy? What in the hell are you doing?"

"Having a baby, silly brother. I'm off to UCLA Medical Center. I've got to go!"

"Roddy!"

"Bye. See you soon."

"Roddy? Damn it!" Steel said, slamming the receiver into place. "It isn't time for that baby to be born yet!"

"They have a way of making up their own minds about those things. Steel, snap out of it. We have to get to the hospital."

"What?"

"Steel!"

"Oh! Yeah, okay. You're coming with me?"

"I'm certainly not staying here alone pacing the floor."

"This is a little scary, Megan. I've never had a baby before."

"You're not the one having it, Uncle Steel. Roddy's the person with the rough night ahead. Come on!"

At the hospital, Megan and Steel were directed to the maternity waiting room. Brian was in with Roddy, the nurse had said, and Roddy's labor was progressing nicely.

"Now what do we do?" Steel said.

"Smoke," Megan said.

"I don't smoke, remember?"

"Pace the floor then. What do they plan to name the baby?"

"Brian wants to name his son, Shield of Courage. His daughter, he says, is to be, Field of Bluebonnet. He's really into this Indian stuff," Steel said, smiling. "Roddy said, 'No way. Waving Goldenrod has spoken.'"

"Field of Bluebonnet," Megan said. "I rather like it." Steel rolled his eyes to the heavens.

An hour later, Megan stifled a giggle as she watched Steel's performance. He paced, sat down, got up again and paced, all in one continuous stream of motion.

"What's so funny?" he asked, glaring at her.

"Nothing. But if you wear out that floor, they're going to send you a bill."

"Fine," he growled, and resumed his pacing.

Two hours passed. Then three.

"What in the hell is taking so long?" Steel said.

"If this is the state you're in as an uncle," Megan said, "I'd hate to see you as the father."

"Megan," he said, "when you have my son, I want you to do it fast, understand? The quicker, the better."

"Yes, sir," she said solemnly. "I certainly will."

"It's a girl!" Brian yelled, bursting into the room. "The most beautiful baby girl you've ever seen."

"It's about time," Steel muttered, then extended his hand to Brian. "Congrats, Dad. How's Roddy?"

"Tired, but okay. She was wonderful, Steel. Talk about brave. Hey, is this Megan?"

"Yes, I am," Megan said, smiling. "Congratulations on your daughter. What are you going to name her?"

"Break it to me gently," Steel said.

"We compromised," Brian said. "Her birth certificate will say Field of Bluebonnet, and we'll call her Bonnie."

"That's lovely," Megan said.

"Steel," Brian said, "I saw my daughter born. She's incredible. Come see my Bonnie."

Megan brushed a tear off her cheek and moved close to Steel's side as he circled her shoulders with his arm. They walked down the hall and arrived at the window just as the curtain was whisked open and a nurse stepped forward to the glass holding a pink-wrapped bundle in her arms.

"I'll be damned," Steel said, his voice strangely husky. "Will you look at her? She's beautiful, so tiny, perfect, like a little doll."

"She's a miniature Roddy," Brian said. "Like the hair? It's sticking up all over the place, black and silky."

"Adorable," Megan sighed, unable to tear her gaze from the sleeping baby. Their child would look like that, hers and Steel's, she thought. It would inherit its father's thick dark hair and bronzed skin. Their son would grow tall, and strong, and proud of his Indian heritage. He would wear the silver hawk with pride. But she must be patient, give Steel the time and space he needed to sort out the turmoil in his mind regarding their future together. He had to find his peace before they could be truly happy. She loved him so much, and because she did, she would wait. She'd drop her pennies in the fountain . . . and wait.

"Bye, Bonnie," Brian said as the curtain was closed. "That is one helluva kid!"

"I'm exhausted," Steel said. "This having-a-baby stuff is hard work."

"No comment," Megan said.

"I'm going to go sit with Roddy for a while," Brian said.

"Tell her hello for us," Steel said. "Night."

In the car, Megan snuggled close to Steel and lay her head on his shoulder.

"Bonnie is such a beautiful baby," she said.

"Small, very small."

"No, she isn't. She's a good size, especially considering she made her debut a bit early."

"Megan, my hand is bigger than her head! I'm not touching her until she grows. A lot!"

Megan laughed softly, and they drove the rest of the way in silence, each lost in their own thoughts.

Their lovemaking in Megan's bed was tender, slow, as they kissed and caressed in a languorous journey of lips and hands. The flame of desire was kindled from a glow to a raging fire that consumed their senses and carried them away to their private place of splendor where they became one. And then they slept; sated, contented, with heads resting on the same pillow.

The next morning, Steel announced that, since Megan was definitely not the maid, it was his turn to cook. The dishes from the previous night were scattered throughout the kitchen due to their hasty departure to the hospital, and Steel simply shoved them out of the way to perform his chores. The meal consisted of runny scrambled eggs, burned toast and bitter coffee. Megan said it was absolutely delicious.

"I have to go home and change," Steel said, pulling her into his arms. "Have a good day and I'll see you tonight. We'll go out to dinner to celebrate Bonnie's arrival. I'll even go so far as to wear a tie. Did I say that? I think my fever is coming back. Seven-thirty?"

"Fine."

"Remember, easy and natural around Clara, okay?"

"Yes."

"Kiss me, Megan James."

"Certainly, Blade of Steel."

The kiss was long and sensuous, and Megan's knees were trembling when Steel finally released her. After Steel left the apartment, Megan had a lovely smile on her face until she went back into the kitchen and viewed the disaster that awaited her.

When Steel entered the police station with a five-foot orange giraffe under his arm, Ginger nearly choked on her coffee.

"You arrested a giraffe?" she teased.

"Like it?" Steel said. "I think it's outstanding. Roddy had a baby girl last night. Field of Bluebonnet Clark alias Bonnie."

"Really? That's super. I'll send her some flowers. Don't you think that giraffe is a bit . . . big?"

"Nope," Steel said, striding down the hall.

When Steel walked into the squad room with the giraffe in tow, no one spoke. No one said a word as he went through the room and down the corridor. Heads turned to watch his departure, shrugs were exchanged, and then everyone got back to work. Steel collected his quart of milk from the kitchen, turned the knob on the office door with his knee and pushed the door open with his foot.

"Hi, Casey," he said. "Oh, good morning, Captain."

"Danner," Captain Meredith said, nodding. "Aren't you going to introduce your friend?"

"It's a giraffe," Steel said, setting it in the center of the room.

"No-o-o," Casey said. "Are you sure?"

"Roddy had a baby girl last night," Steel said, patting the giraffe on the head.

"Hey, that's nice," Casey said.

"That's a pretty big giraffe for a newborn baby," Captain Meredith said. "Are giraffes really that... orange?"

"This one is," Steel said. "Bonnie will love it. Bonnie is short for Field of Bluebonnet. Catchy, huh? Brian insisted she have an Indian name, so they compromised. I have never in my life seen such a tiny kid."

"They grow up all too quickly," the captain said. "Give my regards to Roddy and Brian. Well, back to Bodeen. Casey just brought me up to date. It's quite a setup."

"Yeah," Steel said, taking a swig of milk. "Bodeen overworked his brain this time. It's a slick operation. The only thing we don't know is where he plans to pick up the mirror. I'm guessing he'll break into Memory

Lane at night and make the switch. A tidy break-in, of course.''

"About Megan James," Captain Meredith said.

"What about her?" Steel asked.

"I felt he should know, Steel," Casey said. "I told him that you and Megan are—uh—close."

"So?"

"So, I'm not sure you should stay on this case," Captain Meredith said.

"What in the hell are you saying?" Steel boomed, his jaw tightening.

"Easy, Steel," Casey said.

"Doctors don't operate on their own wives and lovers, Steel," the captain said. "It's the same principle. You could be too close to this, too emotionally involved. If you react as a man instead of a trained police officer, you might blow the whole thing."

"Are you pulling me off this?"

"No," Captain Meredith said. "I'm asking you if I should. People's lives could be at stake here. Megan James is apparently very important to you, and it could cloud your judgment. I'm trusting you, Steel, to be honest with yourself and me."

Steel set the milk carton on the desk and shoved his hands into his back pockets. He turned to look at the smiling giraffe, and a heavy silence fell over the room.

"I love Megan James, Captain," Steel finally said quietly, staring at the giraffe. "I want to be there, close to her, when this thing goes down. I won't allow my feelings for Megan to influence my instincts as a cop because she needs me to have those instincts razor sharp. We're going to get Frankie Bodeen and no one, *no one*, is going to be hurt."

Captain Meredith cleared his throat and started toward the door. "That's good enough for me," he said. "And, Steel?"

"Yeah?"

"I really don't think giraffes are that orange."

"He's a helluva guy, you know that?" Casey said as the door closed behind the captain.

"Yeah, he is. Tough, tough cop. Sure doesn't know beans about giraffes, though."

Casey laughed and shook his head as Steel settled into his chair to polish off the carton of milk. The giraffe just stood in the middle of the room and smiled.

"How," Steel asked, lacing his fingers behind his head, "are we going to cover Megan at the House of Sawyer when she picks up the mirror? I'd bet money Bodeen has a make on us."

"Disguises. Fake beards and bushy eyebrows."

"Give me a break, Jones."

"We'll call in a couple of undercover people who nobody knows."

"Good. Very good, except I want to be there."

"No can do, Steel."

"Yeah, well, beef it up. Two or three guys and a couple of women."

"That's overkill. Nothing is going to happen at the House of Sawyer. The fun begins after Megan picks up the mirror. We have two possible scenarios. Scenario One is if Bodeen pops into Memory Lane to pull the switch, and Scenario Two is if he has Megan deliver it directly to him and he gets sloppy enough to have it in his possession. I can't see him wanting to be anywhere near the two mirrors at once."

"Or, try this one, Casey. He sends someone else into Memory Lane to switch the antiques."

"Trust a hood with two million smackers? No way, Steel."

"Bodeen has a lot of mucho-muscle-no-brain-boys on his payroll. They just do as they're told, no questions asked. A dough head makes the switch, then Megan delivers the crate to Frankie."

"To where? His house? No. That would be dumb. The airport. Yeah, the airport. Hell, that is going to be rough to cover. We'll have to put a mike on Megan."

"I'm hating this, Casey."

"I know, buddy. Think of it as a great story you and Megan can tell your grandchildren."

The expletive Steel said none too quietly caused Casey to cover his heart with his hand.

"Blade of Steel," he yelled, "have you no couth? You never, ever, swear in front of an orange giraffe!"

Steel apologized to the giraffe, then left the office to check the availability of undercover police officers. He and Casey studied the names and made their choices. After getting clearance from Captain Meredith, they left a note in each officer's mailbox to report to Lieutenants Danner and Jones as soon as possible.

"That's under control," Casey said, back in the office. "What's the setup at Memory Lane? Any place to hide in there?"

"I've never been in the back office, and we can't exactly waltz in for a look around with Clara there."

"Well, you'd better call Megan and have her leave the back door unlocked when she leaves today. You and are going for a stroll after dark."

"Oh, great," Steel said, smiling. "There's fancy stuff sitting all over. Just remember, Jones, you break it, you buy it."

"I'll put it on my expense account. Let's go have lunch, then visit Roddy. I want to see the look on her face when she sees that animal."

"Nobody appreciates my giraffe around here," Steel said.

"How did you get it in the car?"

"Its head sticks out the window."

"Ah, man," Casey said. "We are never going to hear the last of this one, Danner. Why do you do these things to me?"

"'Cause I love ya, Jones," Steel said laughing. "Let's go. Our public awaits."

Eleven

Megan glanced at the book again, then squinted at the ceiling.

"Wake up," she said. "*Taatayi*. Watermelon. *Kawayvatnga*. Everyone should know how to wake up a watermelon in Hopi."

Snapping the book closed, she looked at her watch, the telephone, then her watch again. Seven minutes after ten. Steel and Casey were playing burglars at Memory Lane, and she was a wreck. What was taking so long? she wondered. Why hadn't Steel called? How long did it take to case a joint? Was that how they said it?

She pushed herself to her feet and went into the kitchen for a glass of milk, leaning against the counter as she drank it. This was what it would be like being married to Steel, she thought. As his wife, the waiting, wondering, worrying, would all be a part of her life.

Well, so be it. Steel's wife. It sounded glorious. It was a breath away from being reality because Steel loved her and wanted to marry her. Her!

The ringing of the telephone woke Megan from her reverie and sent her hurrying into the living room to answer it with a quick greeting.

"Hi, babe," Steel said.

"Hi," she said, an instant smile on her face as she sat on the sofa. "How's the cloak and dagger business?"

"A bit frustrating, but we figured it out. There's nowhere to lurk in the shadows inside Memory Lane, so we'll have to go with a stakeout. Not wonderful, but it will do. That's what took so long. We had to check out the roof, alley, access streets, the whole bit. Oh, we locked the store when we left."

"Did you break anything?"

"We cleaned it up. Swept all the pieces into the trash."

"What? Oh, no!"

"I'm kidding!" Steel said, laughing. "Honest."

"That wasn't funny, Blade of Steel. I should punch you in the *waakasi*."

"That means cow."

"No, it's watermelon. Isn't it? Darn it. Hopi is a tough language."

"You're learning Hopi? I'll teach you the dirty words."

"Really?"

"No! Well, my *naawakna*, I'm beat. I'm sorry about having to cancel our dinner. We'll go tomorrow night, okay?"

"Fine. Sleep well, Steel. I love you."

"Ditto. See ya."

Megan slowly replaced the receiver and pictured Steel in her mind, allowing his handsome image to fill her mental vision.

"Naawakna?" she said suddenly. "What does that mean?" Flipping through the book, she ran her finger down the vocabulary list and smiled in delight. *Love.*

The next morning, Steel and Casey began the tedious, detailed task of planning the strategy that would catch Frankie Bodeen with the stolen gems in his possession. A squad of junior detectives was assigned to the lieutenants, and endless hours were spent in the following days going over and over the various options.

Alternate plans were constructed to hopefully include all the possible delivery sites of the mirror. Maps were drawn of the areas surrounding Memory Lane and Bodeen's house. Another was made of the airport, and men were given specific locations to cover. When everyone agreed the operation was airtight, Steel insisted they go over it again, and then once more. Casey voiced no objection.

The men assigned to watch Megan while she picked up the mirror at the House of Sawyer started avoiding Steel, so they wouldn't be quizzed yet again on their assignments.

The days passed.

And Blade of Steel Danner had a constant frown on his face.

The night before Megan was to pick up the mirror, she sat on her sofa and watched Steel pace restlessly around the living room. A gentle smile formed on her lips as she saw the furrowed brow, the set of his jaw, the tight coil of his entire body.

The panther, she thought. The sleek, graceful animal ready to unleash its power and strength on its prey, that was Blade of Steel Danner. He had been preoccupied and moody for days, irritable and quick to lose his temper. And she loved him with every breath in her body.

As Steel had grown more tense, Megan had gone in the opposite emotional direction. She was calm, relaxed, and smiled her way through the trying days and nights. She refused to dwell on the approaching caper, as she referred to it in her mind, and simply went blissfully about her business. Steel Danner was, she decided, a powder keg of dynamite about to explode, and if she became frightened and tense, she could very well light his fuse! And so she smiled, mentally placing herself in Steel's safekeeping.

Each morning in the park, Megan dropped her penny in the fountain. As it skittered to the bottom to rest among the hundreds of others, she made her wish. From her heart, from her mind, from the very recesses of her soul, came the hope that Steel would reach out his hand and pull her to his side forever. To be Steel Danner's wife and the mother of his child was her wish, her prayer.

"Steel," Megan asked, focusing her attention on the situation at hand. "would you like something to drink?"

"What? Sure. Fine."

"Coffee? Scotch? Shoe polish?"

"Whatever you're having."

"White shoe polish, or brown?"

"I don't care."

"Steel Danner," Megan said, as she laughed, getting to her feet and halting his flight across the floor, "you're losing it."

"Huh?"

"You have to relax. You weren't this bad the night Bonnie was born."

"Damn it, Megan, tomorrow is the pickup!"

"It is? Well, golly gee, I forgot. I knew there was something I had to do. I'm certainly glad you reminded me."

"Would you knock it off?"

"No! Steel, look at yourself. If one of your men was this uptight, would you leave him on the case?"

"Well, I—"

"Would you?"

"No," he said, raking his hand through his hair. "I'd pull him so fast his head would spin. You're right, I'm not in good shape."

"Nothing is going to go wrong, Steel."

"Oh, Megan," he said, pulling her roughly into his arms, "I love you. When the time comes for me to be there for you in this, I'll be fine, I promise you that."

"I know you will, Steel. I've never doubted it."

"It will all be over soon, Megan, and then..."

Steel stopped speaking as he lowered his head to claim Megan's mouth in a long, searing kiss. And then... what? her mind screamed. He'd look deep within himself for the answers to his questions regarding their future and find what? A directive to leave her? Leave her alone, and lonely, and crying so many, many tears?

"Oh, Megan," Steel said, lifting his head and sinking his hands into her hair as he gazed down at her, "I'm sorry I've been so hard to live with the past couple of weeks. You've been so patient, understanding, and I don't deserve it. All I've done is growl at you."

"Yep," she said, smiling up at him.

"Forgive me?"

"Nope."

"No?" he said, laughing. "That's great. Now what do I do?"

"You should make it up to me."

"How would you suggest I do that?"

"Oh, you'll think of something," she said, starting to unbutton his shirt.

"I've got it! I'll get you a giraffe like Bonnie's. They had one that was bright blue with yellow spots and—"

"Okay," she said, backing out of his arms, "its a deal. It's been nice talking to you, Steel."

With a throaty chuckle, Steel swept her into his arms and strode into the bedroom, where he set her on her feet. With almost agonizing slowness, he drew her sweater over her head and dropped it on the floor, followed by her filmy bra. As he cupped the lush fullness of her breasts in his hands and brought his mouth to their honeyed warmth, Megan tilted her head back and closed her eyes to receive every sensation that rocketed through her.

Steel drew first one then the other rosy bud into his mouth, his flickering tongue bringing each to a taut button. And then he moved lower, inching Megan's jeans down her slender hips and legs, kissing her softness as it came into his smoldering view. She was trembling, awash with desire, and when Steel stood again to claim her mouth she nearly went limp in his arms.

He swept back the blankets and lifted her onto the cool sheets, then stripped off his clothes and stretched out next to her. His hands and lips conducted a lambent journey over her lissome form. His muscles trembled as he held himself back, stroking, kissing her until her passion soared and she moaned from the need of him.

"Steel, please," she gasped.

"Soon, babe. This is for you. You."

Megan wanted to tell him that she would give to him what he was giving to her, but only his name came from her lips as his hand moved to the heated core of her femininity. Sensations swept through her as she moved restlessly under his foray, clutching his shoulders in a viselike grip.

"Oh, Steel, please!"

"Yes, Megan," he said, his voice raspy. "Yes!"

And then they were one. Steel came to her with power, strength, tempered with infinite gentleness, and Megan arched her back to meet him, to bring him closer, fill her, consume her. Their rhythmic motions were in perfect synchronization as they climbed higher and higher, seeking their goal, heartbeats thundering, and bodies glistening.

"Steel!" Megan said as she burst upon the treasured place.

"My Megan," he groaned as the spasms shook him and he shuddered above her.

Steel's strength was drained, and he collapsed against her, his voice caressing her name in a hoarse whisper. He pushed himself up to rest on his arms and kissed her deeply before slowly, reluctantly, moving away and pulling her to his side. For several minutes they remained quiet as breathing and heartbeats returned to normal levels. Their bodies cooled, and Steel reached to draw the blankets over them.

Megan nestled close to him, relishing his heat and aroma, and she sighed as a delicious inertia settled over her. "Cancel the giraffe," she said dreamily, not fighting the somnolence that crept over her.

Steel chuckled and wove his fingers through her strawberry-blond hair, letting it slide like silken threads from his grasp. Within minutes Megan was asleep, and in the glow of the dim light on the nightstand, Steel gazed at her, edging her even closer to his warmth. His frown returned as he watched her peaceful slumber, and the knot in his stomach twisted like a knife.

He loved this woman with an intensity, a depth, he would have never imagined possible. She was beyond the scope of any fleeting, whimsical image he might have had in his mind of the one he never really expected to find. She was everything. Much more than even a million wishful pennies in a fountain could bring.

In that moment when he had assured Megan that the nightmare of Bodeen would soon be finished, he had started to speak of the future, of what they would have when the onus of the situation at hand had been removed. "And then," he had said. And then, what? It was still a hazy blur of unknowns and unanswered questions. In the past two weeks he had pushed it to the back of his mind and concentrated only on formulating the intricate plans for Megan's safety. But it was all there waiting for him, and he would have to make a decision. Soon.

The thought of leaving Megan was crushing, painful. But the scenario in his mind of her grief and long, lonely hours should he lose his life was even more depleting as it hammered against his sense of right and wrong. He felt beaten, weary, as he struggled against the turmoil raging within him. But, no, he mustn't dwell on it now. Every facet of his mind had to be directed toward the ensuing hours that would force Megan into danger, bring her face to face with Frankie Bodeen.

Trying not to disturb Megan, Steel moved slowly off the bed and pulled on his clothes. He'd told her he couldn't spend the night, wouldn't risk being close to her in the morning on the chance that Bodeen's men were watching her activities on the day the mirror would be picked up. He stood staring down at her for a long moment, then after drawing a shuddering breath, turned and strode out of the apartment, shutting the door quietly behind him.

The next morning, Megan was in the royal-blue dress she'd agreed to wear. Steel had taken pictures of her in the bright creation and had given them to the officers protecting her at the auctioning house. She had not been told their identities so as not to inadvertently be searching for them and draw attention to their existence. Her hands were trembling slightly as she sipped her coffee, and she gave herself a firm mental lecture on the necessity of appearing relaxed and carefree.

Just before ten o'clock, Megan pulled open the double doors and entered the House of Sawyer.

"She's there by now, Casey," Steel said, staring out of the office window.

"Yep."

"That Sawyer jerk planned an auction for the same time as the scheduled pickups with the hope that the dealers would buy more stuff."

"I know that, Steel."

"I'm hating this, Jones."

"I know that, Danner. This part is a breeze. The rough stuff comes later."

"Yeah, but I'll be there then. It's this sitting around that's driving me up the wall."

"There won't be any mistakes, Steel. None."

Steel nodded, paced the floor, then returned to the window where he braced his hands on the frame and stared out at the smog-laden city beyond.

At one o'clock Megan walked through the park with the twelve-inch-square wooden box held tightly in her arms. She glanced wistfully at the fountain but continued her journey across the street to Memory Lane.

"Hi, Clara," she said brightly as she entered the store. "You won't have to eat your brown-bag lunch after all."

"Mission accomplished?" Clara asked.

"Yes, I have Mr. Sands's Henri DuPont mirror. He must be such a romantic man. Think of all the fuss he's going to to make his wife happy."

"He's something all right," Clara said quietly. "Megan, I . . . I just wanted to thank you for being so nice to me. You're a very trusting person and have gone out of your way for me. Megan, listen, I've got to tell you something. Mr. Sands is—"

"Hello, Megan darling," a woman said, bustling in the door. "What divine new things do you have for me to see?"

"Lots of stuff," Megan said absently, still looking at Clara.

"I'll go to lunch," Clara said.

"Why don't we talk first in my office?" Megan suggested.

"No! No, I mean, I'm hungry, really starved. I gotta go," Clara said, heading for the door.

"Megan," the woman said sternly, "I do not like to be kept waiting!"

"What? Oh, I'm sorry. Let me put this box away and I'll show you the most divine crystal saltcellars. Absolutely, positively divine!"

"I certainly hope so," the woman sniffed.

Megan hurried into her office and placed the wooden crate on the desk. She glanced longingly at the telephone, wanting desperately to call Steel, but first she had to take care of Mrs. Hoity-Toity. Clara, she thought. Clara had been about to say something about Frank Sands.

"Mee-gan!" the woman yelled. "I'll be late for my beauty parlor appointment if you don't wait on me right this minute."

"Stuff it," Megan said under her breath. "Coming, darling," she said ever so sweetly.

Steel had refused to leave the office for lunch so Casey had gone out and gotten hamburgers and french fries, which Steel ate without tasting.

"Howdy, bosses," a man said, coming into the office. "Megan call? She's back at Memory Lane safe and sound."

"Are you sure?" Steel said, getting to his feet.

"Yes, Lieutenant," the man sighed, "I'm sure. Cross my heart and hope to die. We had to suffer through some auctioning hoopla, then they announced that the dealers could pick up the stuff they'd already bought in Paris. Megan chatted with a few people she knew and went back to the store. She was loose, smiled a lot, did great. No sweat. Clara came barreling out a few minutes later and Thompson is tailing her. Some rich-type woman went in the store, so that's probably why Megan couldn't call yet. Steel, Phase One is A-OK. Your lady came through like a pro."

"Thanks, Bill," Steel said. "I mean that."

"No prob. We'll be on standby, ready to go, for Phase Two. Man, I'm famished. They served cucumber sandwiches at that place. Gross. Later, Lieutenants."

"See ya," Steel said, sinking back into his chair.

"Feel better now?" Casey asked, tapping the bottom of his cup to loosen the ice.

"Yeah, I guess so. Okay, phone, do your thing."

"Thy master's voice has spoken!" Casey said as the telephone shrilled its summons.

"Danner," Steel said, snatching up the receiver.

"Megan James here, sir. I'm reporting in to the commander-in-chief."

"Hi, babe," Steel said, letting out a deep breath. Casey crunched on his ice and smiled. "Word is you did fantastic."

"Piece of cake. Is that right? Or is it, a piece of pie?"

"Cake. You've got the mirror documented for clearance to go back out of the country?"

"Yes, everything was done at the House of Sawyer. Steel, Clara was acting strangely before she went to lunch. She thanked me for being so nice to her. I got the distinct impression she was saying goodbye. Then she started to say something about Frank Sands, but we were interrupted by a customer."

"Well, don't worry about it. Maybe Clara actually had a case of the guilts for helping to set you up. We have a man tailing her. Don't be surprised if she doesn't come back. Okay, next shot is to hear from Bodeen. I'll call you once an hour through the afternoon. If there's someone there, just pretend I'm a customer."

"All right."

"Enjoy the cucumber sandwiches?"

"Your people certainly give detailed reports," Megan said, laughing. "Yes, as a matter of fact, they were quite tasty."

"Grim. I'll talk to you soon. I love you, Megan."

"I love you, too. Bye Steel."

"Oh-h-h," Casey moaned. "It's enough to bring tears to my eyes. He actually said he loved her. There's hope for you yet, Danner."

"Quit chomping on that ice. It gets on my nerves."

"Everything gets on your nerves these days."

"Yeah, I'm sorry about that. I'll go fill Captain Meredith in on where we stand so far."

"Don't tell *him* he gets on your nerves."

"He owes me for criticizing my outstanding orange giraffe," Steel said, striding to the door on his long legs.

Megan called Mrs. Morrison and rattled off a prerehearsed speech stating that the Henri DuPont mirror had been broken in shipping. Mrs. Morrison wailed in dismay, then in the next breath stated that none of her friends were impressed by the purchase of the mirror anyway and would Megan check to see if any memorabilia from Elvis Presley's estate was being released for sale? Megan silently blessed eccentric little old ladies.

Before Steel could make his first check-in call to Megan, she picked up the ringing telephone to hear the voice of Frank Sands.

"How are you, my dear?" he asked.

"Very well, thank you."

"I assume everything went as planned at the auctioning house?"

"Yes, I have the Henri DuPont mirror sitting right here on my desk. It's crated and documented to leave the country."

"Excellent. My wife is going to be delighted with her gift."

"You're certainly a very thoughtful husband, Mr. Sands," Megan said, rolling her eyes to the heavens.

"I try. Now then, about delivery to me. I'm really quite pressed as I have business meetings right up until the moment I leave for Greece. I'll pay you an extra bonus if you'll bring the crate to the airport tomorrow night."

"Well, that's a bit unusual, but yes, all right."

"Good. Drive to the west end of the airport to Private Hangar Number Two. I have a plane there. Say, nine o'clock?"

"Fine, but what shall I do with the mirror in the meantime?"

"It's on your desk? Simply leave it there. Things sitting out in the open give the impression of not having much value. Actually, it doesn't except for the fact that it will make my wife so very happy. So, until tomorrow night, my dear. I'll give you your money when you deliver the mirror."

"Certainly, Mr. Sands."

"Goodbye, my dear."

"Goodbye," Megan said, replacing the receiver. Oh, dear heaven, it was terrible! she thought wildly. Nine o'clock at night at the deserted end of the airport where it was dark and spooky. How were Steel and Casey going to be there without being seen? Frank Sands had said to leave the crate on her desk. He was certainly making sure he knew where it was to pull the switch. If Bodeen came to Memory Lane himself, Steel could grab him and it would all be over. Who was she kidding? Frankie Bodeen had gofers for jobs like that. No, she'd have to keep the rendezvous at the airport. She didn't want to go! "Oh, Lord," she yelled as the ringing of the telephone made her jump. "Memory Lane."

"Steel. Are you alone?"

"Yes."

"Clara is at the bus station, suitcase in hand. She's on her way out of town, it would seem. She—"

"Steel," Megan interrupted. "Frank Sands called already. Oh, God, Steel, I'm starting to get scared."

"Easy, babe. Just tell me what he said."

Megan quickly related the conversation she'd had with Frank Sands and hoped her voice wasn't as shaky as it sounded to her own ears.

"Okay, Megan," Steel said calmly for Megan's benefit, though inwardly he was raging, "leave the crate right where it is. Go home on time and stay put. A policewoman will show up at your apartment about eight saying she's selling cosmetics. Let her in and she'll show you how to use the microphone you'll be wearing to the airport. I can't come anywhere near you tonight, babe, but I'll try to call. I can't promise, though, because I'll be on stakeout at Memory Lane. Megan, don't worry, okay? Nothing is going to happen to you. Nothing!"

"All right, Steel. I think I'm going to deserve my blue giraffe after all."

"You've got it. I love you, Megan. It's almost over. Just hang in there."

"I will. Be careful, Steel. I love you so much."

"See ya," he said, hanging up the receiver and turning to Casey. "It's as crummy as it can get, Jones. Let's round everyone up. We've got work to do."

At midnight Steel spoke quietly into the walkie-talkie and received status reports from the other men staking out Memory Lane. All said the same thing. There was no sign of activity near the store. Steel and Casey sat in their car, which was parked at the end of the alley behind the store. A huge trash dumpster hid them from view, but Steel could see the stakeout by sitting close to the door. Other officers were stationed on the roofs of the adjoining buildings, and the front was covered by two men hidden in the park.

"Well," Casey said, "I don't like this. If Bodeen isn't going to pull a switch here, he'll do it in midair on that plane. We can't storm the plane for search-and-seizure because Megan would be in the line of traffic. Hell, even if we go in early, Bodeen will claim the stuff was planted and his fast-mouthed lawyer will get him off. I swear, Steel, if he—"

"Hold it," Steel said. "We have company. A milk truck just pulled up behind the store."

"A milk truck? That's corny."

"Okay, boys, heads up," Steel said into the walkie-talkie. "No one moves unless I give the word. If it's Bodeen himself, get ready to hustle your butts."

"Roger," a voice said.

"Hell," Steel said, "the milkman is about six-two and skinny as a rail. It's definitely not Bodeen."

"Does he have a package?"

"Yep, and it's sure as hell not cottage cheese. He's pulling the switch, Casey, and that leaves Megan going to the airport tomorrow night. What's the latest on Clara Bodeen?"

"Our guys are sticking like glue. They'll pick her up as soon as they get the word. You know this joker here?"

"Just a sec. He's coming out of the shadows. Hell, its Slats McPhee. Dumb as a post, but one of the slickest break-in boys around when he's not in the clink. The back door and the crate will be easy pickings for him."

"For this I got a sore butt sitting here for hours?"

"Duvall," Steel said into the walkie-talkie. "That's Slats McPhee going into Memory Lane. He just became your best friend. Tail him when he leaves and don't lose him. We'll get word to you when we want him brought in. Call in later with your location and someone will relieve you. Got it?"

"Roger."

"The rest of you," Steel said, "stay put for fifteen minutes after the milk truck leaves. I hope you all enjoyed your evening on the town."

"So much for Phase Two," Casey said. "All the chips are in one pot now. Tomorrow night. Nine o'clock. That's when we play the big one. All or nothing."

"Casey, there's just something wrong here," Steel said. "I can't put my finger on it, but I've got that gut feeling that we're missing a piece of the puzzle."

"Like what? We've been over it all a hundred times."

"Bodeen gave Megan specific instructions as to which hangar to go to."

"Well, yeah, how else is she supposed to find him?"

"True, but that's like putting out a neon sign saying, 'Here I am. This is my plane.' Bodeen is too slick for that. He doesn't advertise. Man, what if he's blowing smoke?"

"He's got no reason to distrust Megan."

"Bodeen stays out of jail by not trusting anyone. He could have purposely given her that information because it's wrong."

"Then how in the hell is she going to find him?"

"I don't know. I've got to think this through."

"You do much more thinking you're going to blow a gasket in your brain."

"I'm telling you, something isn't right!" Steel insisted, then suddenly tensed. "The milkman just left."

"Ol' Slats is speed itself," Casey commented. "Fifteen minutes and we go home."

"Casey, concentrate on what I'm saying." Steel continued while watching Slats slink back to his truck and drive away. "We figure we have it covered, but if we're wrong Megan could be in real trouble. We're going over it again in the morning. Every detail!"

Twelve

At eight o'clock the next night, Megan inspected her appearance in the mirror. Her eyes looked as big as saucers, and no amount of pinching could bring any color to her pale cheeks. Dressed in dark slacks and a bright yellow sweater, her head was covered in a silk scarf to conceal the wire of the speaker leading from her ear to the button-sized device attached to her bra. The microphone had been sewn into the knot of the scarf tied under her chin.

She lay on the bed and drew a steadying breath. She was frightened, *terribly* frightened, she thought miserably. The day had been so long, and each time Steel had called her he had sounded more tense. She knew how concerned he was, and she had tried desperately to keep a lightness in her voice. It was almost over now. Almost. All she had to do was hand the crate to Frank Sands and then the nightmare would be over.

"So do it!" she said, getting to her feet.

At the airport, Steel and Casey sat on wooden boxes in a windowed toolshed located close to the three private hangars. Casey completed a check-in by walkie-talkie to the other officers scattered around the area. Two were in coveralls leaning casually against the outside of Hangar Two, smoking cigarettes and chatting. Two more were inside the hangar sweeping the floor with large push brooms. Four additional men were in the shadows by Hangars One and Three.

At five minutes after eight a pilot appeared in Hangar Two, nodded absently to the working men, then climbed into the cockpit of the small plane. A short time later the engine came alive, and the plane rolled out of the hangar and taxied to the airstrip beyond, where it sat with lights blinking, ready for flight.

"Damn," Steel said. "I don't like this. He's a hundred yards away."

"Relax, Steel," Casey said. "You're about to jump out of your shorts."

"Casey," the walkie-talkie squawked, "this is Duvall. There's a plane backing out of Hangar Three."

"Okay, we see it," Casey said.

"We don't need extra company," Steel said. "That guy is going beyond Bodeen's plane and... Hell, he's just sitting there, too."

"Maybe he's waiting for clearance from the tower," Casey said.

"Maybe, but I don't think that's it. Something isn't right here."

"Damn it, Danner, you've been harping on that all day. We've been over it so many times I could do this in my sleep. Just zip it, will ya?"

"I've got this gut feeling that— Hold it, here comes a limo. Look at that, Casey. It's Bodeen, big as life. He's walking toward the plane and his muscle man is going into the hangar. The car is leaving."

"Yep," Casey said. "The players are on stage. Interesting. Bodeen is apparently going to wait outside the plane. Heads up, Steel. Megan just drove up."

"I'm hating this, Casey."

"Hang in there, buddy. Switch on the transmitter."

Megan turned off the ignition and jumped in surprise as Steel's voice came over the tiny speaker in her ear.

"Megan? It's Steel. Can you hear me?"

"Yes."

"How are you doing, babe?"

"Fine. Really, I'm fine."

"Okay. We're all here, Megan. There's nothing to worry about. Take the box and walk into the hangar. Bodeen's man is in there. With any luck he'll take it from you. If he does, get the hell out of there."

"All right, Steel."

"Try to appear relaxed, casual, if you can. Don't look around at any of the workers in there. They're our men, and we don't want any attention drawn to them. Go on, babe. Get out of the car."

"Yes, I'm going."

Megan got out of the car, shifted the strap of her purse to her shoulder and reached back to lift the wooden box off the seat. Willing her feet to move one in front of the other, she approached the brightly lit hangar and entered. An enormous man in a dark suit was standing in the middle of the area, and Megan had the irrational thought that he looked like a direct descendant of King Kong.

"Hi," she said brightly, stopping in front of him. "I'm here to deliver this to Mr. Sands. Do you work for him? I guess I can give it to you."

"No," the man said, in the form of a deep growl. "He wants you to take it out to the plane."

"Damn," Steel said in Megan's ear.

"What plane?" Megan questioned.

"That one out there. You'll get your money from Mr. Sands."

"Well, I declare," Megan said, "I have to hike all the way out there? I certainly hope I'm getting a nice bonus for this."

"Just get movin', lady."

"Don't be rude," Megan said, marching past him in a huff.

"Beautiful, babe, beautiful," Steel said. "It's almost over. Nice and easy now. Just stroll on out there."

"My knees are shaking, Steel," Megan whispered.

"You look gorgeous. I love you, Megan."

"Oh, how sweet. Do I get my blue giraffe for this?"

"You bet. Quiet now. You're getting close."

"Damn it!" Casey said. "Steel, you were right! It's a setup! The limo is coming from behind that second plane. The one Bodeen is in front of is a decoy. He's going to take off in the other one!"

"Good evening, my dear," Frankie Bodeen said to Megan. "I assume that's the DuPont mirror?"

"Yes, it is. It's lovely, and I hope your wife enjoys owning it."

"I'm sure she will. If you'll just give it to me, I have your money right here."

"Stall him, Megan!" Steel said. "Stall! Give the word, Casey. Let's move in!"

"Now, Mr. Sands," Megan said, "it's part of my service to instruct you on the proper care of your mirror. You must clean all the little crevices with...a toothbrush. Yes, a toothbrush and warm, soapy water. Then pat it dry with—''

"Damn it, woman," Bodeen roared, "give me that box!"

Megan gasped as Bodeen tore the crate from her arms. As she turned she saw Steel, Casey and a crowd of other men thundering toward them as a huge car approached from the opposite direction. In the distance she could see a small plane, and suddenly everything became crystal clear.

Bodeen was going to escape! her mind screamed. He wasn't getting on this plane; he was going on the other one, and the car would whisk him out there before Steel could catch him!

"Stop!" Megan yelled. "You rotten bum, you don't play fair!"

The car came to a screeching halt, and Frankie took off in its direction.

"No!" Megan shrieked.

Shaking with anger, Megan reached in her purse and grabbed the coin bag full of pennies. Then she whipped her arm around and flung the pennies as hard as she could at Frankie. They sprayed over him and hit the pavement like copper raindrops.

In seemingly slow motion, Bodeen skidded on the shiny metal and flipped into the air, landing with a resounding thud on his back. The crate catapulted upward and smashed on the ground, splintering into pieces, the mirror breaking on impact. The stolen jewels scattered across the pavement in twinkling rainbow colors.

"Megan!" Steel yelled.

With a screech of tires, the car sped away, missing Megan only by inches.

"You'll pay for this!" Frankie bellowed, struggling to his feet. "All of you! I'll get you! I swear I'll—"

"Can it, Bodeen," Casey said. "The ball game is over."

"Megan!" Steel said, running to her and pulling her roughly into his arms. "Oh, God, Megan," he said, holding her so tightly she could hardly breathe.

"My pennies," she mumbled into Steel's sweater. "Those are my pennies for the wishing fountain. I've got to go get them."

"Hey, I'll buy you a thousand shiny new ones," Steel said. "Come on, let's get you out of here."

"Man," Casey said, coming to where they stood, "you should see those gems. What a haul. Megan, you were something."

"Nice going, Megan," Duvall called. "Want to join the force?"

"Hey, Megan," another officer said, "tell Steel you're after his job."

"I'll finish up here," Casey said. "The uniforms got the limo and our guys snagged the ape in the hangar. There's a squad car on its way here. They'll haul ol' Frankie downtown. I'll have Clara and Slats McPhee picked up. We did it. We got Bodeen. I can't believe it. Your lady is a heroine, Steel. Why don't you take her home?"

"I sure would like to pick up my pennies," Megan said, frowning.

"I'll get you, Danner," Bodeen yelled. "You and Jones are finished. I've got connections that you know nothin' about."

Steel looked over at Frankie, then walked slowly in his direction.

"Easy, Steel," Casey said. "Don't blow it now."

"Oh, Lord," Megan whispered.

Steel stared down at Frankie Bodeen, and the hood-lum seemed to shrink under his icy scrutiny. Frankie stepped backward into the two men standing guard over him.

"You messed with Steel's lady, Bodeen," Duvall said, shaking his head. "You really shouldn't have done that. Know what Indians do to people who hassle their women? Man, it's unreal."

"Don't touch me, Danner," Frankie said. "I've got witnesses. I'll sue."

"Steel," Megan said quietly, "would...would you help me pick up my pennies? How can I wish in the fountain without my pennies? Please, Steel?"

Steel seemed to snap out of a semi-trance as he heard Megan's softly spoken words. He drew a deep breath and shoved his hands into his pockets.

"There are people waiting for you in prison that you've ripped off in the past, Bodeen," Steel said. "Enjoy your stay. Get him out of here, Duvall."

"You bet," Duvall said, grabbing the back of Frankie's jacket and propelling him toward the patrol car.

Steel walked back to Megan and circled her shoulders tightly with his arm.

"See ya, Jones," he said, his voice hushed.

"Nighty night, Danner," Casey said. "Bye, Megan."

"Good night, Casey."

Steel led Megan through the hangar and to her car where he opened the passenger door for her. As she moved to enter, he pulled her to him, holding her against the rock-hard wall of his chest.

"Are you all right?" he asked, his voice husky with emotion. "Are you, Megan?"

"Yes, I'm fine. I was scared to death, but I knew you wouldn't let anything happen to me."

"What made you throw those pennies? Lord, it was brilliant."

"I don't know. I just suddenly realized that Bodeen was going to get away. I was so angry I didn't even stop to think about what I was doing. I was great, huh? Think I should join the police force?"

"No!" Steel said, turning her around and shuffling her onto the seat. "My heart couldn't stand the strain. Your cop career is over, Miss James."

"Well, darn," she said as he closed the door. And her next career? she thought. Would it be as Steel's wife? The mother of his baby? Would it? Or was Memory Lane all she was to have? Frankie Bodeen was out of their lives. Now Steel would bring to the front of his mind the questions and doubts about their future together. And all her pennies for the wishing fountain were gone.

"Give me your keys," Steel said, sliding behind the wheel.

Steel drove away from the airport as Megan pulled the scarf from her head and removed the transmitter from her ear and bra. She leaned her head against the headrest of the seat and closed her eyes as a wave of utter fatigue swept over her.

"You'll sleep like a log," Steel said. "You've had quite a night. I'll take you home and put you to bed."

"Will you stay?"

"There's nowhere else I want to be, babe," he said quietly, brushing his thumb over her cheek.

It was all a blur to Megan. She was vaguely aware of Steel leading her into her apartment and removing her clothes. A soft nightie was floated over her head, and Steel was talking about emotional aftershock, which made no sense at all. He told her he loved her and that brought a crooked smile to her lips. With a sigh of contentment, she snuggled against her pillow and closed her eyes.

"Aren't you coming to bed?" she asked, then yawned.

"Soon. I'll be right here, Megan."

"I love you, Steel."

"Yeah, babe, I know. Go to sleep."

Steel sat in the chair and gazed at Megan as her breathing became deep and regular in a matter of moments. Leaning forward, he rested his elbows on his knees and made a steeple of his fingers.

It was over, he thought. Bodeen was in jail. Months and months of tedious work and it had finally paid off. There they had been, a squad of great big, tough cops, and Bodeen had been snared by a handful of pennies tossed by a whisper of a girl. Incredible. Damn, Megan had nearly been hit by that car when... No, no sense dwelling on it now. It was finished. Done. And Megan was safe. She'd been great, so brave, and he loved her.

"I do love you, babe," he said quietly as his eyes lingered on the sleeping woman. And so? Now what? he wondered. He and Casey would be assigned to a new case and life would go on. The demons in his mind could no longer be ignored. There had been no time to dwell on his inner turmoil as he'd worked out the endless details surrounding Megan's meeting with Bodeen. But now the decks were clear and he had to face the foe head on.

Steel pushed himself to his feet and walked to the edge of the bed. He pulled the blanket carefully over Megan's shoulders, then gently trailed his thumb over the soft skin of her cheek before turning and going into the living room. He paced the floor in long, heavy strides as a multitude of voices screamed in his mind.

Then slowly, slowly, the jumbled mass began to become clear as Steel sifted through each piece of the puzzle in turn. He recalled the years he had spent trying to protect Roddy from her wild life-style, then remembered the words his sister had spoken that day he had stopped in for lunch. Roddy had chosen the path Brian had offered her. Roddy had known her own mind, what her needs and wants were. Steel had hovered over her, yet the final decisions had been hers to make.

Megan had also spoken to him, but had he listened, really listened? As he had with Roddy, Steel was now trying to protect Megan from a way of life *he* was passing judgment on, with little regard for Megan's wishes. She accepted his world with its dangers and unknowns, and he had not respected her enough to believe in her ability to realize her own strengths. He had taken it upon himself to decide their future, and he had no right to do that.

Steel knew he wanted Megan as his wife. He knew he wanted a son to give the silver hawk to. He knew *his* happiness depended on having Megan at his side. He'd made his choices, determined his needs. To not allow Megan the same freedom to make decisions regarding her own existence was wrong. Very, very wrong.

He would ask Megan James to marry him, Steel thought, taking a shuddering breath. He would mentally toss a million pennies in the fountain and wish, pray, she would agree to be his wife. The shadows in his soul were gone. He was at last at peace. The final step was up to Megan.

"I love you, babe," Steel said to the silence. "I need you, Megan."

A wave of fatigue washed over him, and he shut off the light and returned to the bedroom. After tugging off his shoes, he stretched out fully clothed on top of the spread. He was tense, tight, and he willed his muscles to relax and allow him to sleep and end the grueling day. Finally he sectioned off his mind and drifted away to Arizona as a boy on his pony until exhaustion claimed him and he slept.

Steel woke before dawn and ran his hand over his beard-roughened face. He needed a shower, shave, clean clothes and three or four cups of coffee. He also needed, he thought, to wake Megan and ask her to marry him! No, that wasn't fair. She needed her rest after the ordeal she'd been through.

Steel swung off the bed and went into the bathroom. A shower held no appeal with no clean clothes to change into, and he returned to the bedroom to gaze at Megan, who was sleeping peacefully. Checking the clock, he set the alarm so she'd have plenty of time to get to Memory Lane. In the living room, he scribbled a note saying he was going home to clean up, then had to report into work. He'd talk to her later, he wrote, and signed it, "I love you. S." After calling for a taxi, Steel propped the paper against the telephone, retrieved his gun from the end table and left the apartment.

Several hours later, Casey let out a sigh and tossed his pen on the stack of paper covering his desk.

"Arresting a guy is easier than the paperwork you have to do to document it," he said.

"No joke," Steel said, scrawling his name on the bottom of a form. "I hate this garbage. Duvall said Clara Bodeen has signed statements tying Bodeen into the whole scam. The ape-man in the hangar is talking, too. Bodeen is in for a long stretch in jail."

"Poor baby," Casey said. "So, how's Megan this morning? Recovered from playing cops with us?"

"She was still sleeping when I left. It hit her last night on the way home. She just spaced out."

"That's normal. She sure was great, Steel. Man, what a number with those pennies. Oh, I gave instructions that Megan's pennies were to be picked up along with the gems and she'll be getting them back. They seem to mean a lot to her."

"That's nice, Casey. Thanks. She has this wishing fountain where she drops in a penny every morning and...well, she'll be very pleased."

"Steel, you and Megan are so good together. You're still not struggling over this thing about your maybe being killed, are you?"

"No," Steel said. "I pushed it away during this bit with Bodeen, but it came back on me last night like a ton of bricks. I sorted it all out and I'm going to ask Megan to marry me."

"I'll be damned," Casey said, grinning. "That's great! Fantastic!"

"Not if she says, no."

"Fat chance. She loves you, Danner. I have no idea why, but she does. Hey, man, I'm happy for you."

"Thanks. I'll feel better when I hear her agree to the whole thing."

"There they are," Captain Meredith said, coming into the office, "Flash and Dash. Congratulations, Lieutenants. It was a helluva job. I did hear, however, that the collar really belongs to a little lady with a fist-full of pennies."

"Yep," Steel said, "Megan got Bodeen."

"She'll be receiving an official certificate of appreciation from the department," the captain said, "but tell her for me that I think she's quite a woman."

"I will," Steel said, nodding, "and she is."

"So marry her, Danner," the captain said as he lef
the room, "before somebody else does."

"I'm trying to!" Steel yelled after him.

In the early afternoon, Megan looked up to see a
enormous blue giraffe coming in the door of Memor
Lane.

"Oh, it's beautiful!" she said as she laughed, throw
ing her arms around Steel's neck. "Thank you."

"You earned it," he said and kissed her quickly, the
smiled down at her. "And this jar contains all of th
pennies you clobbered Bodeen with. These are compli
ments of Lieutenant Casey Jones."

"Oh, how sweet. What a lovely thing for him to do.'

"How are you, babe?" Steel said, a frown now on hi
face.

"I'm fine. I sure was flaky last night, I guess, but
was good as new when I woke up."

"Great. Here, let's put this animal in your office be
fore one of your society ladies comes in and flips out.
need to talk to you, too, Megan."

"Yes, all right," she said, a knot tightening in he
stomach.

In the office, Steel set the huge toy in the corner an
absently patted it on the head before turning to fac
Megan. He shoved his hands into the back pockets o
his jeans, palms out, then took a deep breath before at
tempting to speak.

"Megan," he said, his voice hushed, "you know tha
I love you, don't you?"

"Yes," she said, wrapping her trembling hand
around her elbows, "and I love you."

"You also know I was having a real problem wit
asking you to become my wife because of this gun
carry and all that it entails. I've looked deep inside my

self and I realize that I was being terribly unfair to you. I dismissed everything you said and took it upon myself to make your decisions for you. I had no right to do that.''

"Steel, what are you..."

"Megan, I..." Steel paused, took a deep breath, then wiped a line of perspiration off his brow with his thumb. "Megan, I don't have a crystal ball to look into the future and know what it will bring. I only know I love you, want you, need you with me. Will you marry me? Will you, Megan? Please?"

"Oh, yes, Steel!" Megan said, running into his arms. "Yes! I was so afraid you'd decide that we shouldn't be married. Steel, I love you so much," she said, tears spilling down her cheeks.

"Oh, thank God," he said, his mouth melting over hers.

The kiss was long and powerful. It spoke of love, of commitment, of forever. It sealed the promise of a future that would be celebrated one day at a time with peace and happiness.

"Megan," Steel asked, when he finally lifted his head, "would you come to Arizona with me to meet my grandfather? It would mean a great deal to me."

"Yes, of course, I will."

"I'll take you there... as my wife."

A multicolored sunset streaked across the Arizona sky in hues of purple, orange and yellow as Steel and Megan approached the adobe house. They stopped for a moment to drink in the beauty of the heavens, then Steel's ebony eyes swept over the land where he had been born and become a man. It had been here at the knee of his grandfather that Blade of Steel Danner had learned of his proud heritage and been taught the laws of honesty and truth. And it was here that he had returned with the only woman he had ever loved.

"Would you mind waiting here just for a minute, Megan?" he asked.

"Fine," she said, smiling at him.

Steel moved slowly forward as he saw the silhouette of his grandfather outlined against the darkening sky. Steel walked toward the old man, whose face was turned to the departing sun.

"Blade of Steel," his grandfather said, not turning in Steel's direction. "You have come. *Um waynuma?*"

"I have come, Grandfather."

"You bring news of Waving Goldenrod? Of Brian? Of Field of Bluebonnet?"

"They're fine. I bring their love. You have a strong, healthy grandchild."

"It is good," he said, slowly moving to face Steel. "The night casts shadows on your body, but still I see your eyes of many faces. You are filled with joy, Blade of Steel. Your soul is at peace."

"Yes, Grandfather," Steel said, a catch in his voice, "I have brought my woman, my wife, to you, to this land."

"It is good, Blade of Steel. Come."

Megan chewed nervously on the inside of her cheek as the two men approached. Chief Danner stopped in front of her and looked directly into her green eyes. She met his gaze steadily as silent seconds ticked away.

Then Chief Danner nodded. "Welcome, my daughter," he said. "You bring happiness to my heart and to the heart of my grandson. My home is yours."

"Thank you," she said, smiling at him. "Thank you so much."

Inside the immaculate house, Chief Danner made a fire in the hearth and then served up three plates of stew from the small stove. Steel whispered that his grandfather would not speak during the meal and they ate in silence. The time for talking was later. When the meal was completed, the dishes washed and Chief Danner sat in his rocker by the fire, he waved Steel and Megan into the chairs opposite.

"Do you wish to have a son to pass on the silver hawk to?" Chief Danner asked. "You want this woman to bear your child?"

"Yes, I do," Steel said, grinning at a blushing Megan.

"You are a warrior who goes into battle," the chief said, "and must go alone. There were many warriors in the early tribes of our people. They fought bravely and came home to rest at the breasts of their women. Now, at last, you have your woman."

"I had many doubts, Grandfather. I questioned my right to bring my woman into a warrior's world. It was Megan's strength that gave me the courage."

"If the doubts plague you again," the old man said, "you must think of, *'Iisaw Niqw Pu Tsirot.'*"

"The story of 'The Coyote and the Birds?'" Steel asked, frowning.

"Many times as you grew up I told you that Hopi legend. Do you remember it?"

"Yeah, sure. The coyote wanted to fly when he saw the mother bird teaching her children. The baby birds each gave the coyote a feather and said he could fly if he tried, and he did. Then the birds flew up and pulled the feathers out of his fur, and the coyote fell to the ground and died."

"That is right. How do you see the legend, Blade of Steel?"

"The coyote tried to be a part of a world he didn't belong in. When he realized that, it destroyed him."

"That is not how I see the legend," Chief Danner said. "I view the coyote as brave, very brave. Above all odds he jumped from the tree and flew. But then he grew careless and did not protect his feathers from those who wished him ill. He could have stayed in his new world had he cherished his gifts. A wife, a son, are precious treasures, Blade of Steel. You are a warrior, but also a man. You must protect yourself in battle to the best of your ability. Use your strength in your wars, your gentleness at the breast of your woman. Protect the feathers of love and keep safe what is yours. If you had sacrificed your heart for the cold metal of your weapon, your soul would be empty."

"You have great wisdom, Chief Danner," Steel said quietly, turning to smile at Megan.

"I have lived many years, Blade of Steel. Remember the coyote. Protect what is yours. I have spoken."

"And I...have listened," Steel said, tears blurring his vision.

"I love you, Steel," Megan whispered.

Chief Danner nodded slowly several times, then got to his feet and walked into the bedroom and closed the door.

"And I love you, Megan Danner," Steel said, covering her lips with his.

Megan locked the front door of the store and walked across the street to the park. Stopping in front of the fountain, she took a penny from her purse and held it tightly in her hand. Suddenly the water rippled as a cascade of pennies fell into the water, and Megan looked up in surprise.

"Steel!" she gasped. "I thought you had to work late."

"On our two-week anniversary? Nope. All those pennies I tossed in there represent how many wishes I have. That's how much I want. I want you, your love, forever. I want our child. I love you, Megan. With every breath in my body, I love you."

"And I love you so much," she said, moving into his embrace to be held tightly by strong arms. "I love you, Blade of Steel. Let's go home."

"We have to make a stop on the way."

"Oh? What for?"

"A goldfish in a pretty bowl with marbles on the bottom," Steel said, circling her shoulders with his arm as they started away.

"That was one of my wishes."

"I know."

"And the others? The dog, the cat, the... Oh, Steel, all I need is you."

"I'm going to see to it that all your wishes come true, Megan."

"When we buy the goldfish I want to get a piggy bank," she said.

"Why?"

"Because I won't be throwing my pennies in the fountain anymore. Every dream, every wish in my heart has come true."

"It is good," Steel said nodding. "We have spoken."

At the edge of the park, they turned and looked at the fountain of wishes, then smiled at each other before continuing on their way. Steel pulled Megan close to his side, and she relished his strength and warmth.

They were together, and there was nowhere else they wished to be.

AMERICAN TRIBUTE

Where a man's dreams count for more than his parentage...

Look for these upcoming titles under the Special Edition American Tribute banner.

CHEROKEE FIRE
Gena Dalton #307—May 1986
It was Sabrina Dante's silver spoon that Cherokee cowboy Jarod Redfeather couldn't trust. The two lovers came from opposite worlds, but Jarod's Indian heritage taught them to overcome their differences.

NOBODY'S FOOL
Renee Roszel #313—June 1986
Everyone bet that Martin Dante and Cara Torrence would get together. But Martin wasn't putting any money down, and Cara was out to prove that she was nobody's fool.

MISTY MORNINGS, MAGIC NIGHTS
Ada Steward #319—July 1986
The last thing Carole Stockton wanted was to fall in love with another politician, especially Donnelly Wakefield. But under a blanket of secrecy, far from the campaign spotlights, their love became a powerful force.

AM-TRIB-1R

AMERICAN TRIBUTE

American Tribute titles now available:

RIGHT BEHIND THE RAIN
Elaine Camp #301—April 1986
The difficulty of coping with her brother's
death brought reporter Raleigh Torrence
to the office of Evan Younger, a police
psychologist. He helped her to deal with
her feelings and emotions, including love.

THIS LONG WINTER PAST
Jeanne Stephens #295—March 1986
Detective Cody Wakefield checked out
Assistant District Attorney Liann McDowell,
but only in his leisure time. For it was the
danger of Cody's job that caused Liann to
shy away.

LOVE'S HAUNTING REFRAIN
Ada Steward #289—February 1986
For thirty years a deep dark secret kept them
apart—King Stockton made his millions while
his wife, Amelia, held everything together.
Now could they tell their secret, could they
admit their love?

 **Silhouette Desire**

COMING
NEXT MONTH

GREEN FIRE—Stephanie James
Was Rani's life endangered by inheriting an antique emerald ring? It
was a fake—but the man who appeared on her doorstep was
undeniably real. He claimed he was there to protect her....

DESIGNING HEART—Laurel Evans
Lighting director Stella Ridgeway was perfectly content with her
career; playwright Sam Forster was quite happy being alone. But
there was an undeniable magnetism between them that neither
could resist!

BEFORE THE WIND—Leslie Davis Guccione
Disheartened after a bad marriage, Whitney was determined to avoid
the pain of involvement again—until she met Paul. Paul helped her
regain her self-esteem, but could she learn to love once more?

WILLING SPIRIT—Erin Ross
Athena MacKay went to Scotland to reclaim Kildrurry, "haunted"
castle of her ancestors that had been stolen by the Burke clan.
Christopher Burke was no ghost—but could she give her heart to
the enemy?

THE BLOND CHAMELEON—Barbara Turner
Delancey was good at impersonating movie stars—and good at hiding
her real self from the man she loved. But Stuart was intrigued, and
insisted on finding the woman within.

CAJUN SUMMER—Maura Seger
Eight years ago, Arlette left the Louisiana bayou to pursue her own
career. That had meant leaving Julian behind. Now she was back, and
this time he wasn't going to let her go!

AVAILABLE THIS MONTH: